APACHE ATTACK!

Ki did what the Apache would never have suspected. He threw himself forward, the iron-hard edge of his hand slashing downward to connect with the base of the Apache's thick neck. He tasted the Indian's foul breath, saw his eyes roll upward, and then he gave the Indian a hip-throw that brought him down hard in the dirt. Ki dropped one knee on the man's chest and snatched up the Bowie to place it at the Indian's throat. . . .

*   *   *

SPECIAL PREVIEW!

**Turn to the back of this book for a sneak-peek excerpt
from the exciting, brand new Western series . . .**

FURY

. . . the blazing story of a gunfighting legend.

-*- WESLEY ELLIS -*-

LONE STAR

AND THE MEXICAN MUSKETS

JOVE BOOKS, NEW YORK

LONE STAR AND THE MEXICAN MUSKETS

A Jove Book / published by arrangement with
the author

PRINTING HISTORY
Jove edition / July 1992

ISBN: 0–515–10881–2

Jove Books are published by The Berkley Publishing Group,
200 Madison Avenue, New York, New York 10016.
The name "JOVE" and the "J" logo
are trademarks belonging to Jove Publications, Inc.

PRINTED IN THE UNITED STATES OF AMERICA

10 9 8 7 6 5 4 3 2 1

LONE STAR

AND THE
MEXICAN MUSKETS

Chapter 1

The Concord stage was dusty and crowded as it rolled across the vast Sonoran Desert toward Tucson, Arizona. Jessica Starbuck's green eyes were closed, and she tried to shut out the unpleasantness of the rough, hot ride. Let's see, she thought, one more stage stop at Gila Crossing and then just four more hours across this miserable desert and they would arrive in Tucson.

"Some water?" Ki asked, holding up a canteen.

"No, thanks," Jessie said, opening her eyes and smiling at the samurai.

"We ought to be arriving at Gila Crossing soon. I remember they have the sweetest well in the entire Sonoran Desert."

Ki nodded and placed the canteen between them. He was dressed in his usual samurai clothing, which consisted of a loose black tunic and matching pants. He wore sandals and gave the impression of being a large Chinaman. Actually, Ki was the son of an American seaman and a Japanese woman of some nobility. He had been born and raised in Japan, where he'd learned his skills as a master of the martial arts, of *te*, or hand and kick fighting, and also the use of the samurai's traditional weapons.

"Maybe you'd rather drink some of my whiskey," a rough, dirty man across from them offered.

"No, thank you," Jessie replied.

The man raised his bottle and drank in big gulps. "Ahhh," he said, smacking his lips and grinning boldly at Jessie. "I think a little whiskey would sure lighten up the conversation in here somewhat. Don't you agree, Miss Starbuck?"

"No."

The man's smile faded. His name was Mace Bow and he was a horse trader on his way to Yuma. When he'd boarded this stage puffing a large cigar, Jessie had insisted that he put the thing out because its stench was so powerful as to make her stomach flop. There had been some words about that, but in the end, Bow had hurled the cigar out the window.

"Now, Missy," he said, "I think, seeing as how we are going to travel all the way to Yuma, that it's high time we got acquainted. I realize that I'm not clean and pretty like your Chinaman servant or some of the men you probably associate with, but I'm a *real* man. Might be that you and I could have some fun together."

Jessie felt the samurai stiffen in anger, and before he made a move against the fool opposite her, Jessie touched his arm.

"It's all right, Ki. I'm sure that Mr. Bow means no disrespect." She looked at the rough man. "Do you?"

"Aw, hell no!" Bow snorted, glancing at the other passengers. "I was just thinking that, since I got more whiskey than I need to get drunk on, I'd be a gentleman and pass this bottle around. It'd help lighten things up considerably, I reckon."

"Well," the fourth passenger, a smallish, middle-aged shopkeeper from Yuma named Arnold Gilliam, said, "I don't partake of spirits, sir. And frankly, I'd prefer that you didn't either. Company policy on this line forbids drunkenness."

Bow twisted around and stared menacingly at Gilliam until the much smaller man squirmed and became frightened.

"I think," Bow said, "that you are an impertinent little son of a bitch who needs a lesson in manners."

2

Before Jessie or Ki realized it, Bow had grabbed the man's face, pinched his thumb and forefinger deeply into Gilliam's cheeks, forcing his mouth open, then rammed his whiskey bottle down the storekeeper's throat and poured.

"Stop it!" Jessie cried as the little man choked in terror.

Ki had seen enough. The iron-hard edge of his hand slashed downward to strike Bow on the forearm with a powerful *teganta* blow.

"Oww!" the big man shouted as the bottle fell to the floor and began to empty itself between their feet. "Damn you!"

Bow lunged forward, but before his broad fanny left the seat cushion, Ki struck again, and this time the edge of his hand connected solidly at the base of the horse trader's thick neck. Bow's bloodshot eyes rolled up into his skull and his entire body shivered before he collapsed against the little storekeeper.

"Oh God!" the little man from Yuma cried, pushing Bow off him and spitting whiskey. "Now he really will kill us!"

"No he won't," Jessie said. "In fact, I'm going to insist that he be removed from our coach when we reach Gila Crossing. The man is foul and ill-mannered. I won't have him in the same coach with us."

"But what if they refuse?" Gilliam asked, his face ashen and his voice shaking with fear. "After all, he has a ticket for Yuma."

Jessie's eyes flashed with anger. "I'll buy his ticket myself if necessary. But he won't ride another mile past Gila Crossing with us, that much I will promise you, Mr. Gilliam."

The storekeeper nodded. He had recoiled as far from Bow as he could get, hugging the coach wall in fear. His eyes went to the samurai. "Mister, you better hope he don't wake up and go for his gun. And he will if he ever sees you again."

"If he does," Ki said, "then he will have to die."

Gilliam blinked and swallowed. "I don't know how you did that," he said, "but all my life I've wished that I could protect

3

myself against bullies like him. And now you just hit him with the edge of your hand as if it were an ax or something and he is out cold. How?"

"It's a form of hand fighting that I have practiced for many years," Ki explained patiently. "It's a matter of timing, balance, and mental attitude."

A glaze of incomprehension crossed Gilliam's eyes. "I guess it must be," he said, nodding his head. "Well, I just have one piece of advice—don't ever try that against a man with a gun or a knife. You do, you'll die. I promise that much."

Ki nodded. The samurai understood that the little store-keeper was simply trying to repay a favor by warning him about men like Mace Bow, who would bully and then kill without giving the matter a second thought.

"I will be careful," Ki promised.

Gilliam's coat front was drenched with spilled whiskey, and now that he was beginning to calm down, he must have realized that he was a mess. Removing a handkerchief from his pocket, he dabbed at his coat and looked to Jessie.

"I have a family," he said. "I've been married for sixteen years now. Martha helps me in the store. I think you'd like her."

"I'm sure I would," Jessie said pleasantly.

"We . . . we do just fine in our little business. And if either you or your friend, Mr. Ki, need anything—anything at all—I'd sell it to you at cost. Just sort of in appreciation for what you did just now."

"That's very generous of you," Jessie said, "but I think we've got everything we need for our trip to San Francisco already taken care of."

"May I inquire as to the nature of your travel?"

"Business," Jessie said, not wishing to elaborate. "I have business in San Diego first, then in Los Angeles and finally San Francisco."

"Oh," Gilliam said. "Martha and I were in San Diego once. It was a beautiful place. We wanted to move there, but . . . well, we didn't know anyone and we are doing well in Yuma. It's just that it is so hot in the summer."

"I know," Jessie said, judging the temperature in their coach to be over one hundred degrees.

"Where are you from?" Gilliam asked, looking at them both.

The man was talking too much, and Jessie knew it was because he was still shaken by the traumatic experience he'd just undergone. So she told him that she and Ki were from Texas.

"My father left me a nice cattle ranch in the southwest part of the state," she said. "But he also left a number of businesses that I oversee and whose offices are headquartered in San Francisco."

Gilliam nodded. "That's . . . that's *VERY* impressive, Miss Starbuck. Very impressive. Me, now, I'm just a little guy. But it sounds like you—"

"Gila Crossin' comin' up!" the driver shouted. "Get ready to step down and stretch your legs."

Jessie smiled at the storekeeper and began to gather her belongings. They had not had a stop for nearly six hours, and she was very eager to get out of this hot box and stretch. They would have a meal here and it would probably be poor fare, just as were most of the meals they'd had at this long string of stage stops. Usually, you got beef, beans, and tortillas. Sometimes there might be a little corn or even some dessert, but not often.

"I'm starved," Gilliam said. "Martha is a wonderful cook. Say, doesn't this stage hold over for the night in Yuma?"

"Yes," Jessie said, "I believe it does."

"Well you and Mr. Ki could come have dinner with us tonight." Gilliam's eyes grew excited. "I know the missus wouldn't mind such short notice. We could talk business and maybe you'd even want to invest in Yuma."

"Maybe another time," Jessie said. "We're tired and dirty. I think a nice hotel room, bath, and early to bed is what we'd prefer."

Gilliam's face dropped. "Oh. Of course. I should have guessed that."

The man looked so disappointed that Jessie said, "Perhaps we will have time to visit your store in Yuma before we leave. There might be something that we need to purchase."

Gilliam brightened. "At cost. I insist on that, Miss Starbuck. Same for you, Mr. Ki."

"Thank you," the samurai said.

"Wonderful!" Gilliam exclaimed. "You'll really appreciate the selection of clothing that Martha and I stock. You might even decide to trade those little slippers for a pair of good boots or those black pajamas for—"

Ki was spared further ignorance because Mace Bow groaned and stirred.

"Oh my Lord!" Gilliam cried, his face going pale again. "What are we going to do! He's waking up!"

Jessie looked sideways at the samurai. "Perhaps it would be best if we tied the man up until we leave. That way, you could eat and I could rest without worrying that he'd try something else stupid enough to get hurt."

Ki nodded with agreement. Between his feet on the floor was a leather satchel that held a few of his martial arts weapons. Among them was a black cord useful in many ways. Ki removed the cord and expertly bound Mace Bow's hands, behind his back, and then his feet.

Gilliam was so frightened that he even tested the knots to make sure that Bow could not work them loose.

"I sure hope you can make the stationmaster agree that this man is a danger to all of us and has to be removed."

6

"I will make him see the light of reason," Jessie said with assurance. She might have to pay the stationmaster a few dollars, but if that's what it took, that would be far preferable to having to share another mile in the same coach with the vile horse trader.

"I just thank heavens that you two are riding with me," Gilliam said, mopping his brow. "If I'd have been alone with that man . . . well, I fear he might have taken my life. I'm carrying quite a lot of cash, you see."

Jessie thought the small man a fool to mention that fact to anyone, but she did not say so.

"You have nothing to fear," she said. "And I'm sure that the remainder of our trip will be far more pleasant without Mace Bow."

"I'm sure it will be too," Gilliam said, pulling back the leather curtains and eating dust in order to look ahead toward Gila Crossing.

A few minutes later, the coach rolled to a halt at the stage stop. Jessie saw that another stage had arrived before them, and its passengers were standing around under the shade of a rickety porch while several sweat-drenched men tried to repair the coach's axle.

"What happened?" their own driver shouted.

"We had Indian trouble about eight miles to the west of here," the other driver grunted. "Had to drive the coach off the road because the damned Apache had dragged rocks across it. Cracked the axle going around, but they'd have had us dead to rights if I'd stopped. Tell you all about it before you leave."

"Oh Lord!" Gilliam cried. "Did you hear that! Apaches are on the warpath again! And they're just up ahead."

Gilliam looked as if he might faint. Jessie glanced at Ki, and the samurai's expression was grim but composed. They had fought Indians together before, and it was not an experience that they ever hoped to repeat.

7

"Maybe we'll have to stay here a few days until we get an army escort," Gilliam blurted. "They do that sometimes when it's bad with the Apache."

Jessie sighed and pushed open the door as the coach ground to a stop. The Gila Crossing station was a hovel in hell and the last thing she wanted was to remain here a few days waiting for the cavalry.

Still, it was better than the horror of being captured by the bloodthirsty Apache.

Chapter 2

"Miss Jessica Starbuck, I believe," a well-modulated voice said, causing Jessie to turn around.

"Why, Mr. Lamont!" she said with genuine pleasure as she extended her hand to the tall, distinguished old gentleman. "What a surprise and delight to find you here!"

"I wish that I were anyplace but Gila Crossing," the man confessed with a wink. "But as long as I'm forced to be here, I can't think of anyone that could dress up this hellish place as you can, Jessie."

"Still the flatterer," Jessie said, noting how Alton Lamont III had aged quite drastically since she'd seen him five years earlier. He seemed a little bent and there was a cloud of pain in his eyes, but his voice was strong and his handshake as firm and confident as always.

"When a man loses appreciation of beautiful women, fast horses, and good brandy," Lamont said, "he might as well write his own obituary. And I am not quite ready to do that."

"What are you doing here?" Jessie asked.

"Urgent business," the rich old man confessed. "I have to reach El Paso in a hurry and—as I'm sure you are sadly aware—this is still the fastest conveyance available. But I swear I will never ride another stage again!"

"I'm about to make the same pledge," Jessie said as they moved over to the shade of the station, where they could get reacquainted. "I understand that you had Indian trouble."

"Yes," Lamont said. "Fortunately, the hardcases I was forced to share my coach with are excellent marksmen. Otherwise, I think we would have been Apache bait by now."

"How many attacked the coach?"

Lamont frowned. "At least twenty. The shotgun guard is wounded and being tended to inside the station. Several of us passengers were nicked by bullets or arrows—the Indians used both."

"But you're unscathed."

"Of course," Lamont said, brightening. "I have always been extraordinarily lucky that way. My heart, eyes, lungs and . . . well, plumbing are in an advanced state of decay, but my luck holds."

Jessie laughed softly. The man was not called "Lucky Lamont" for nothing. He'd struck it rich in the California gold fields and then gone over to the Comstock Lode ten or twelve years later and made another huge strike. Alton Lamont III was said to be worth three million dollars, and for more than forty years, he'd been a womanizer, a philanthropist, and the toast of San Francisco.

"And what about you?" Lamont said. "Surely you could have found a more comfortable conveyance."

"Of course, but I was also in a hurry," Jessie admitted. "Besides, I have to go to San Diego and Los Angeles before continuing on to San Francisco. It just made good sense to take the stage. But that was before I learned that the Apache were on the warpath again."

"And there will be no cavalry, I'm afraid," Lamont said. "I know that because I ran into the officer in charge of the fort at Yuma. He told me they were having Paiute troubles."

"So we're on our own."

"I'm afraid so," Lamont said, his expression grim. "If it wasn't for the fact that I'm in such a damned all-fired hurry, I would suggest we both stay here until help arrives."

Jessie looked around at the station. It was very grim. "The samurai and I will take our chances on the stage."

"I'm sure that you will be just fine," Lamont said, gazing around. "I haven't seen your samurai."

"There he is now," Jessie said as Ki dragged the inert body of Mace Bow around the stage, attracting the attention of everyone stranded at the station.

"My," Lamont said with a chuckle, "that man of yours will never change. Who's the unfortunate victim this time?"

"He's an uncouth brute that I'd planned to put on *your* stage going back east," Jessie confessed.

Lamont's craggy expression grew pained. "I've got three others just like him already. Please don't do that to me."

Jessie took mercy on the man. "Very well. I'll have him bound and tied up on the roof."

"The sun will broil him alive," Lamont said.

"Hmmm," Jessie mused. "I guess you're probably right about that. Besides, if we're attacked by Apache, we'll need all the help we can get."

"There's someone I'm traveling with that I want you to meet," the old man said. "Come along for a moment."

Jessie followed him around the station tender's shack and out to the corral, where a tall, slender young man of about nineteen was standing among the horses.

"Juara?" Lamont called.

The young man turned around, and Jessie realized at once that he was a half-breed.

"Juara Madrid, I want you to meet the daughter of a very old and cherished friend of mine. This is Miss Jessica Starbuck of Texas."

11

The youth seemed to look through Jessie for a moment before he left his horses and came over to extend his hand. When he spoke, his voice was strong and his English almost faultless. "My pleasure, Miss Starbuck."

Jessie smiled. "And mine as well," she said, feeling a strong attraction to the tall, handsome young man.

"Juara's father was an employee of mine," Lamont explained. "He grew up among his mother's band of the Apache. Now that his mother has died, Juara is accompanying me to El Paso. He wants to raise fine horses and we are going to look at a ranch. Juara has a way with horses, Jessie. I've never seen anyone who could gentle them like this young man."

Juara Madrid's cheeks flushed with embarrassment. "Horses trust me," he admitted almost shyly.

"You're being too modest," Lamont said. "You've earned my trust as well, and that isn't easy. I expect that you'll be supplying horses to stage lines like this one in the years to come."

When Juara said nothing, Jessie touched his arm. "I wish you great success in your work. And if you ever get a little deeper into Texas, please stop by my Circle Star Ranch. It would be a pleasure to have you as a guest. I'm always looking for men who can handle wild horses."

"I'll remember that," Juara promised before he turned back to the horses.

Jessie watched the half-breed approach a stallion that was snorting and stamping. It was the kind of horse that looked dangerous, but the half-breed just held out his hand and the horse quickly grew calm.

"He does have a way with horses," Jessie said as she and Alton Lamont walked back toward the station.

"He is a remarkable horseman," Lamont said. "His mother, I understand, was a great horsewoman. Anyway, I met the boy several years back and each time I'd pass through this country,

12

he'd greet me and show me a trick or two with horses."

"Both his parents are dead?"

"Yes," Lamont said. "His father was a most valuable employee and friend. I promised the man on his deathbed that I'd help his son get a start in the horse business."

So, Jessie thought, that explained it. Alton Lamont never made a promise he could or would not keep. His handshake was his bond, and deals worth millions were sealed on it without even the mention of a contract.

At the corner of the station, Lamont stopped and looked back at the young man. "He got into a little trouble after his mother died. That's one of the reasons that I've got to be in El Paso on Friday. You see, I'm guaranteeing his good behavior and taking responsibility. Otherwise, he might have to go to prison."

"What did he do?"

"He beat a lawman half to death. Way I hear it, the lawman raped an Apache girl and Juara was the first to avenge the act."

Jessie nodded. "I see. If the so-called lawman had raped a white woman, he'd probably have been hanged."

"Undoubtedly," Lamont said, "but you know how certain whites consider all Indians to be less than human beings. They treat them like dogs."

Jessie sighed. "Him being a half-breed and an Apache to boot, I'd expect you might have some trouble with these rough men at this station. I'm sure they would do that young man harm if he even so much as looked at them in the wrong way."

"I know that and that's why Juara is staying out here in the corral. I'll bring him some food before we go. I just hope that people treat a half-breed a little better in Texas than they do in the Arizona and New Mexico territories."

"Some will look past his color, some won't," Jessie said. "It doesn't matter where you go, there are people who hate anyone that looks, dresses, or acts different than themselves. I've seen it a hundred times with Ki."

"Yeah," Lamont said, "I hadn't thought about that. But the samurai is a fighting machine."

"It sounds like Juara Madrid can already handle himself," Jessie said.

"Oh, he can do that, all right. He don't look strong but he's quicker than a cat and tough as manzanita brush. Did you notice that big Bowie knife on his belt?"

"I did."

"He can use it," Lamont said. "They say he's killed several men—all in self-defense. I tell you this—I'd never have wanted to try to go after him, not even in my prime. I'm just glad to have him along for protection."

"Against who? The Apache, or the rough passengers that are traveling with you?"

"Both." Lamont frowned. "I sure wonder if you wouldn't be better off remaining here until the cavalry arrives to escort you and that stage on to Yuma."

"That could be weeks," Jessie said, spotting Ki over by the stage. "Excuse me a moment, please."

Jessie walked back toward Ki. "I've had a change of heart," she told the samurai. "We may need this man's gun if we're attacked."

"What about the cavalry?"

"They're not coming," Jessie said. "If we leave Gila Crossing, we do it without expecting help."

"Your choice, Jessie."

"I vote we leave as soon as possible," Jessie said. "If there are Apache to the west of us, they've probably already scattered and run halfway down to Mexico by now. They never stay in one place more than a day."

"Let's hope you're right about that," Ki said.

From the station came the strident clanging of a dinner bell.

14

"Let's get in there and eat," Jessie said, "because from the looks of this rough crowd, there won't be much in the way of seconds."

Ki nodded with agreement. He dragged Mace Bow over to shade and dumped the man's body before escorting Jessie into the dim stage station.

"Sit down and chow up!" a sweaty, heavyset man ordered as he carried a big black pot of beans from his stove. "There's beef frying and bread cookin' too. Everybody just find a place at the table and help yourself. But no hands in the pot!" the man warned. "Any of you try and scoop food out with your paws, I'll crack your head with a skillet and toss you out to eat scraps with the dogs."

Jessie sat down between Lamont and Ki. She was aware that everyone was staring at her with more hunger than they were the kettle of beans. This was a hard, mostly womanless country, and even plain girls attracted an inordinate amount of attention.

"Gentlemen," Alton Lamont III said. "I think maybe we ought to start eating and stop staring at the lady."

The rough men tore their eyes from Jessie and dug into the kettle of beans as if they were starving. They finished the beans even before the bread and the beef were slapped down on the bare tabletop.

"Wonderful cuisine," Lamont said dryly.

"Huh?" the cook snarled. "You got a complaint, old man?"

Lamont shook his head. He had complaints and could have bought the entire stageline lock, stock, and barrel, but he said nothing except, "Excellent beef, though perhaps a trifle over-seasoned."

The cook scowled. "It's Mexican burro meat, but I marinate it in chili and Tabasco sauce and some other ingredients that I keep to myself. I have to 'cause the meat itself is usually spoiled and you got to kill the rot."

15

"How creative," Lamont said with a gulp as he chewed thoughtfully.

Jessie had been about to stab a steak from the plate but changed her mind. Instead, she waited for the bread to finish being baked, and it was surprisingly good.

The coffee was almost as strong as the beef and beans—you had to strain the chunks of coffee beans with your teeth.

"We got that axle fixed," a big man whose shirt was drenched with sweat said as he tromped into the station and took his place at the end of the table. "But, Homer, you damn sure better stay on the road. That repair job ain't meant to blaze new trails."

"Do my best," a heavyset, chinless man said around a mouthful of food. "Reckon as soon as the hostler gets the team hitched, we ought to be leavin'. We're four hours behind schedule now."

"I've got to be in El Paso by next Friday morning," Lamont said. "And I expect to be there."

The driver did not like the threatening tone of the old man's voice. "Mr. Lamont," he said, "we're all bustin' our asses to keep this stage runnin' on schedule. Way I see it is, we ought to be damned thankful to still be wearin' our hair after that Apache attack."

There wasn't much conversation after that, and when the hostler called out that the eastbound stage was ready to roll, Homer struggled to his feet and started for the door.

"Everybody that's goin' better get to goin'," the cook said. "Homer, he's such an independent son of a bitch that he won't wait a minute on anybody."

Jessie and Ki went outside to bid Alton Lamont farewell and godspeed. The half-breed came up to Jessie and smiled. "I won't forget you," he said in his quiet voice. "You are the most beautiful woman I will ever see."

Jessie's cheeks flamed, but she recovered enough to say, "You've obviously been taking flattery lessons from Mr.

Lamont. Good luck to you, Juara. And don't forget my offer."

Lamont overheard Jessie and stuck his head out the door. "Now don't you try and go hiring him away from me, Jessie! I'm offering him a partnership in a horse ranch."

Jessie laughed and said to the young man, "You'd better accept his offer."

Juara raised her hand, and to everyone's surprise, he kissed it and then climbed into the coach with Lamont and the other three passengers, who did not even attempt to hide their jealous disapproval.

"Hiyahh!" Homer shouted, slapping the lines down hard against the fresh team's rumps.

A moment later, the eastbound stage was disappearing in its own cloud of dust over the very same rough road that Jessie and Ki had just suffered.

Ki watched the stagecoach until it vanished. Jessie said, "You look worried. Is something wrong?"

"No," Ki said after a long pause. "It's just that I had a bad feeling about those three men inside the coach with Mr. Lamont. They had the look of coyotes."

"Yes," Jessie said, "I had the same feeling. Well, between Alton, Juara, and the driver, I think that everything will be all right."

Ki nodded, but his handsome face still reflected deep concern.

Chapter 3

Because Mace Bow was unable to climb up onto the roof of the coach with his hands and ankles tied, Jessie allowed the man to ride in the coach.

"But keep your mouth shut," she warned, "and if you cause any problems, then I'll have Ki deal with you again."

Bow's eyes burned with hatred. "I guess you know," he growled, "that I won't let this pass. I've got as much right to enjoy this stage as the rest of you. I've got a right to talk, smoke, spit, drink, and cuss if I choose."

"Do any of those," Ki warned, "and I'll put you back to sleep."

For just an instant, Jessie thought the big man was going to lunge across the coach and try to throttle Ki. But Bow managed to get his rage under control. "When do I get my gun back?" he asked.

"When we get to Yuma I'll give it to the sheriff," Jessie said. "And I'll tell him that you're a troublemaker and a man to be watched."

Bow snorted with derision. "Miss Starbuck, you haven't a clue as to the kind of trouble I'm going to cause you later. And what about the Apache?"

"If they attack, we'll see," Jessie said.

18

" 'We'll see'?" Bow mimicked. "Why, lady, if we're attacked by Indians, you're going to need all the help you can get. I don't see no gun strapped around the waist of your Chinaman."

Ki said, "Call me a Chinaman again and I'll break your arm."

Bow started to made a crude response, but when he saw how serious Ki was, he fell into a brooding silence.

"Well," Gilliam said, trying to sound cheerful. "I'm sure that we won't have any more trouble. And as for the mis-understanding between us, I think we ought to all just shake hands and be friends."

Gilliam worked up a false smile and stuck his hand out to the sullen horse trader. "What do you say, Mr. Bow? Why don't we shake hands all around and be friends!"

Bow looked down at the proffered hand and then he spat on it.

Gilliam jerked his hand back and tore out his handkerchief. His face was filled with shock and revulsion, but he didn't say anything.

"You are a real son of a bitch, aren't you?" Jessie said to the man across from her. "You don't belong among civilized people."

Bow was smiling triumphantly. "I don't like that weasely little bastard," he said. "And if I took his hand, I'd crush it. Better for him I just spit."

"Oh yeah!" Gilliam cried. "Well, if I were a younger man, I'd . . ."

"You'd still be a chickenshit little coward," Bow said with a sneer. "On the best day of your life I could whip you one-handed."

"That's enough!" Jessie commanded. "One more word and I will ask Ki to silence you for the rest of the way to Yuma."

Bow was smirking as he turned his face to the window. He was the kind of man, Jessie understood, who made himself feel big by bullying and humiliating smaller, weaker men like Arnold Gilliam.

For the next two hours, not a word passed between them, and then the driver up above shouted down. "Riders coming off to our left! I think they're Indians!"

"Oh God!" Gilliam cried, shrinking lower on his seat. "I thought the driver said they'd probably all ride south to Mexico!"

Jessie was nearest to the leather curtain, and she pulled it open and stared through the boiling dust. Across from her, Mace Bow did the same.

"It's Apache!" Bow said. "And they ain't coming to wish us a nice day."

The dust was so thick that Jessie couldn't see clearly, but she estimated that there were at least ten Indians and they were coming fast from about a half mile away.

"I'll need my six-gun," Bow said. "Give it to me!"

Jessie looked at Ki, who shook his head. Jessie said, "Not until we are under attack."

"What!"

"Give it to me," Ki said. He took the gun and shoved it into his waistband. Looking at Bow, he said, "The only way you're going to get this back is if you climb up on the roof with me."

"Are you crazy!"

"Suit yourself," Ki said. "But my weapons are up there and I'm not about to leave you down here with Miss Starbuck."

"Without me in the fight, you and her haven't a chance! That little storekeeper ain't going to be any help. Look at him cringing like a baby!"

"Shut up!" Jessie railed. "Now just do as Ki says. If we die, so do you."

Bow could see the logic in Jessie's warning, and he could tell that she wasn't bluffing about not giving him his gun unless he joined Ki on the roof.

"All right, dammit!" he cried. "Let's get up there! Maybe we can pile some of them mail sacks around us and have some kind of a chance at livin' through this."

"Good luck," Jessie said to the samurai, who threw open the door and climbed out, dragging himself up on top.

For the first time, Mace Bow looked worried, as he hesitated beside the door. He stared out at the fast-approaching Indians and he looked down at the ground, which seemed a blur.

"If I fall, I'll break my neck for sure."

"If you don't get up on top," Jessie shouted, "you'll *wish* yourself a broken neck before the Apache get through torturing you."

"They'll do even worse to you, Miss Starbuck," Bow said with a leer. "They'll all ride your pretty little ass into the dirt."

Jessie wanted to reach out and claw the man's eyes and that leer off his ugly face, but instead she turned her attention to Gilliam.

"Arnold," she said, "you've got to help us."

"But I don't have a gun."

"I've an extra in my bag," Jessie said, digging a pearl-handled Colt from her bag. "It's loaded and it shoots straight. The Apache will most likely split their force and come at us from both sides."

"But . . . but I can't hit anything!"

"Try!" Jessie lowered her voice. Shouting would completely unnerve this man. "Just try," Jessie said calmly. "Even if you miss, it will still help keep them back."

Gilliam nodded. He looked scared half to death and his skin was very pale, but he took the gun and Jessie hoped the little storekeeper would have the presence of mind to use it to good advantage.

Up on the roof, the samurai tore into his own gear and removed from a canvas bag a most unusual-looking bow and quiver of arrows. The bow was constructed of layers of wood glued together and bound at several places with red, silken thread.

"What the hell is that!" Bow cried. "Ain't you got a rifle or anything!"

Ki knelt and strung the bow. He slipped the quiver over his shoulder and drew out an even more unusual-looking arrow. The arrow had a razor-sharp tip, but just behind its steel head was a small ceramic bulb fitted with two holes.

"We're dead men!" Bow shouted to the driver, who had begun to lash his team into a hard run.

"Here," Ki said, handing Bow his pistol. "Don't shoot until they are well within range." Bow leaned over and dragged a couple of mail sacks over. He spread-eagled himself on the top of the roof and licked his lips nervously. "We're dead men," he repeated.

Ki studied the Apache. It was uncommon to see them mounted on horses, because they were most effective fighting on foot. Unlike the Plains Indians, the Apache held the horse in complete disdain. They would ride whatever they could steal or capture until the animals were half-starved by the desert and too weak to travel fast. Then, the Apache would kill their horses and devour them in an orgy of gluttony.

The first Apache opened fire at two hundred yards, but it was a waste of lead and none of the others fired until they'd cut that distance by half.

Bow fired then, but Ki yelled, "Hold your fire! There's no way you can hit one of them at this range."

"I was shooting for their horse!"

Ki got down on bended knees. The coach was rocking so violently that there was a real danger of being bounced off the roof. If the fall didn't kill a man, the Indians would certainly finish the job.

Ki nocked the strange-looking arrow that he called "Death Song." As the Apache drew nearer, several others began to fire their weapons. Ki raised his bow and pulled back the string. The roof of the coach was bouncing them like beads of water on a burning skillet, and it required all of the samurai's concentration to take aim, then fire. The rough horse trader's eyes bugged with amazement to see how Ki's samurai bow spun around in his hand 180 degrees.

Even over the thunder of the coach and pounding of flying hooves, Bow heard the terrible shriek of Death Song as the wind whistled through the little ceramic bulb. Indeed, the shriek seemed to intensify as the arrow reached out and homed in on its target, a lead Apache warrior. And then, just as suddenly as the shriek had begun, it ended as Death Song plunged into the Indian's chest.

"Jaysus!" Bow cried, blinking furiously because he was unable to believe what he'd just witnessed.

Ki nocked a second arrow and fired again as Jessie's six-gun began to crash with authority. Two more Indians cartwheeled over the backs of their ponies and the others let out bloodcurdling cries of anger. The Apache split into two groups and whipped their mounts harder.

Mace Bow was shooting fast but hitting nothing because the roof of the coach was rocking and bucking so violently. He cursed with pain when a bullet ripped through the mail sack and struck him in the shoulder. Ki felt a bullet crease his cheek.

"Ahhh!" the driver cried. He wrapped the lines around his rifle so they wouldn't fall away, then he tried to tear his six-gun free, but another bullet knocked him off his seat. The poor man struck the earth and rolled over and over, yet was still alive.

Ki saw one of the Apache pull his horse up beside the badly wounded driver, who was trying to push himself to

23

his hands and knees. The mounted Apache emptied his gun into the driver's body, bullets pinning the man to the earth. Satisfied, the Apache howled like an animal before rejoining the hunt.

Ki knew that the coach was going to wreck unless he took over as the driver. But to do that meant that he could not use his bow or help in the fight. The samurai knew that he had no choice but to drive, so he threw himself forward and grabbed the lines.

"Keep shooting!" Ki yelled back over his shoulder at Mace Bow.

But Mace seemed paralyzed by fear, or perhaps pain. He clung to the rooftop of the coach, holding his bloody shoulder and sobbing incoherently.

Down below, Jessie was keeping up a steady, deadly fire. Her father had taught her to become expert with both pistol and rifle. Jessie did not hurry her shooting. One by one, she evened the odds until there were only four Apache left in her line of fire.

Behind her, she could hear Arnold Gilliam firing too. She glanced back over her shoulder and saw that the frail storekeeper was holding her pearl-handled pistol in both hands and that each time he pulled the trigger, he would flinch and close his eyes.

"You're doing fine!" Jessie shouted.

Gilliam turned around. "Are we going to make it!"

"Yes!" Jessie cried. "Just . . . Arnold!"

An arrow of all things had struck the poor man in the neck. Gilliam screamed and fell backward, blood pumping from his wound. Jessie tore off her bandana and clamped it around the arrow, hoping to stanch the flow of blood. She could hear the sounds of the Indian ponies almost next to them, and when she glanced up from the wounded man, she saw an Apache through the window.

Jessie fired instinctively and the Indian disappeared.

"Hang on!" she cried to Gilliam. "Can you hold this in place!"

The little storekeeper clamped his own hands around the arrow and the bandana. He was stiff with fear and shaking all over, but he still had enough presence of mind to realize he had to save his own life.

Two more arrows cut through the coach and Jessie twisted around and fired again. The hammer of her six-gun dropped on an empty, so she grabbed the pearl-handled Colt and threw herself back onto the seat just as another Apache appeared. Jessie shot him at almost point-blank range and he vanished.

She was just about to fire at another Apache some distance out when she heard a scream and saw a blur drop past the window. Jessie stuck her head out the window and saw Mace Bow's thick body strike the earth, then roll to a stop. The Apache, decimated in numbers, chose to break off the chase and take their fury out on this last victim.

Jessie saw them leap from their horses, and she almost imagined she heard Mace Bow scream for help, but she pulled her head back inside the coach.

"Arnold," she said, half-expecting that the man would already have bled to death.

His eyes flew open. He swallowed and croaked, "Don't let them capture me alive! I couldn't stand to be tortured. Shoot me, please!"

"They've dropped back," Jessie said. "They've given up the chase because of their losses."

Gilliam stared at her with something very much akin to incomprehension. "Don't lie to me!"

"I'm not lying." Jessie leaned closer. The Apache arrow seemed to be embedded in Gilliam's throat at a downward angle as if it were hugging the man's windpipe.

"You've got a good chance of getting out of this alive,"

Jessie told the man. "If the arrowhead had severed or even nicked the jugular vein, you'd already have bled to death. So just hang on, Arnold, and we'll get you to Yuma and a doctor."

"But what about this arrow!" he exclaimed, holding it steady between his thumb and forefinger so that it did not move. "Are we just going to leave it in me?"

"I don't know yet," Jessie confessed. "Once we put some distance between us and the Apache, we can stop and take a good look. But until then, just hold it real still."

"I will," Gilliam breathed. "Oh God, I will!"

From up above, Ki shouted, "Jessie, are you all right down there!"

"Arnold took an arrow in the neck, Ki! We need to stop as soon as it's safe."

"Right!" came the shout telling Jessie that the samurai would pull the coach in but not until they were out of sight of the Apache.

"Hang on, Arnold. We're only an hour or so to Yuma."

The storekeeper nodded and closed his eyes. "I killed one," he whispered. "I'm not proud of it, but I did what I had to do."

"That's right," Jessie said, smoothing the man's pale forehead. "And I'm proud to have had you fighting at my side, Arnold. Proud as could be. And once your wife and the citizens of Yuma hear about this, you'll become a hero."

Arnold's eyes flew open. "Me? A hero?"

"That's right," Jessie told the little man. "I've never seen a man so cool and deadly under fire as you were just a few minutes ago. Why, I know for a fact that you killed at least *three* Apache."

"Three?"

"Uh-huh," Jessie said. "To be honest with you, I didn't hit that many myself and I'm sure that Ki didn't either. You were the difference in this battle, Arnold. Not Mace Bow or any of the rest of us. It was *you*."

The little man clutched the Apache arrow even tighter. "If I live through this," he grated, "I'm going to keep this arrow as a souvenir and I'll tell this story a thousand times before I grow old."

"You do that," Jessie said, noticing how the bleeding around the shaft of the arrow was beginning to clot. "Because when the chips were down, you were a hero."

Arnold Gilliam's thin, chalky face was transformed by a beatific smile as he closed his eyes and hung on to the Apache arrow and his life.

Chapter 4

Jessie held and offered encouragement to the scared and wounded Arnold Gilliam, while Ki drove the stage on toward Yuma. It was almost sundown before they saw the outline of the old desert town. Yuma had a long and turbulent history. Originally founded on the California side of the Colorado River, it had been a Spanish missionary settlement until the local Indians had revolted and massacred the whites. Later, the Army had founded a post called Fort Yuma, which was supposed to protect travelers bound for California. But the Indians had never accepted the whites, and the Army was almost powerless to stop their frequent depredations.

Fort Yuma became Arizona City and was moved over to the Arizona side of the river, and eventually the name was changed back to Yuma. Now the stagecoach rolled up the dusty road that passed irrigated farmland and small ranches, many owned by Mexicans whose children loved to sit on the fences and wave at the passing stage.

This day, however, Ki had his hands full just handling the team, and when they finally entered the hot, dusty little town itself, the absence of a shotgun guard, at least a half dozen arrows embedded in the stage, and Ki's grim expression caused an immediate stir.

Ki pulled the weary team up to the stage stop and climbed down as men crowded around, all of them asking questions.

"Hold it!" Ki shouted. "We were attacked by Apache about twenty miles to the east and they killed the driver and a passenger. Is there a doctor among you?"

"I'm the town's only doctor," a young man said, detaching himself from the anxious crowd.

"There's a passenger inside and he's badly wounded," Ki said.

At just that moment, Jessie pushed the door open, and at the sight of Arnold Gilliam lying across the seat covered with blood and an arrow protruding from his neck, a woman in the crowd fainted.

"It's his wife," someone said.

"Well, take care of her!" Jessie said angrily. "And some of you help get this man outside."

"No," the doctor said, stepping up to the door. "I think I'd better examine him before we take the risk of moving him to my office."

Jessie realized that this was a good idea. "Come on in," she said. "He's lost blood but not so much that you'd think the arrowhead touched his jugular vein."

"Is he conscious?"

Gilliam opened his eyes. He looked confused and disoriented and his color was very poor. "Martha? Martha!"

"She's all right," Jessie said even as Martha was being attended to.

"My name is Dr. Holt. Don Holt."

Jessie nodded. "This man has been nothing short of courageous," she said loud enough for everyone to hear. "He killed several Apache and we'd never have made it through without him."

"Arnold Gilliam?" a big man asked with obvious surprise.

"Yes," Jessie said. "He's a real hero."

The crowd nodded and pressed closer, but the doctor's full attention was on his patient. "Mr. Gilliam, can you hear me?"

"Yes." Gilliam's voice was very weak.

"It's Dr. Holt. I'm going to remove this bandana and take a closer look at your neck. Just hold still and stay calm."

Gilliam didn't want to let loose of his hold on the Apache arrow, but the doctor finally got him to relax, and when he removed Jessie's bloody bandana, he leaned close to study the wound. He had long, supple fingers and they gently probed around the arrow.

"I can't work in here," the doctor said, straightening. "We've got to get him to my office, where I have my surgical instruments and adequate light."

The doctor looked at Jessie as if seeing her for the first time. "How bad are you hit?" he asked.

Only after the fight had Jessie realized that a bullet had grazed her upper rib cage. "It's just a scratch, I think," she said, fingering the stiff dried blood on her blouse.

"Let's hope so," the doctor said. "I'll want to examine the wound after I'm finished with this man."

Jessie nodded with understanding. "Let's just see if we can save Arnold. He's been hanging on for quite some time."

"He's lucky to be alive," the doctor said, before he turned and called out over his shoulder for help in getting the wounded man out and carried to his office.

There was no shortage of volunteers who wanted to help carry Arnold Gilliam. The man's poor wife revived just as her husband was being carried past her, and at the sight of his pale face and bloodstained clothes, Mrs. Gilliam promptly fainted again.

"Just make her comfortable," the doctor shouted as he supervised the handling of his patient. "And for crying out loud, tell her right away that her husband is still alive and we're going to do everything we can to keep him that way."

"Did poor old Arnold really kill a couple of Apache?" someone asked Jessie as they hurried off toward the doctor's office.

"He sure did!"

"Well I'll be damned. Who'd ever have figured Arnold a hero."

Jessie pushed past with Ki leading the way, and the entire crowd followed except for a few women who stayed by Mrs. Gilliam until she regained consciousness.

"Ease him down on that examination table and everyone clear out," Dr. Holt ordered.

"You might need some help," Jessie said. "I'm volunteering."

"You look like you ought to be my patient rather than my assistant," the doctor said. "But all right."

"Ki," Jessie said, "why don't you stand by the door and keep everyone at bay except Mrs. Gilliam?"

The samurai understood and ushered the curious outside, answering all their rapid-fire questions.

Dr. Holt was efficient. He rolled up his sleeves, washed his hands, and then laid out a half-dozen surgical instruments.

"Mr. Gilliam, are you still awake?"

This time, the storekeeper didn't answer. The doctor grabbed his wrist and closed his eyes for a moment. "Pulse is weak and racing. The heart is overtaxed and trying to pump enough blood to the organs to keep everything operating. I need to get that arrow out of there in a hurry. Can't afford to lose much more blood."

Jessie realized that the young doctor was talking to himself, rather than her. She watched as he selected a scalpel.

"I'm going to have to make a small incision in order to pull the arrowhead out. If it won't retract, then I'll have to make

31

an excision on the posterior of the neck and push the arrow on through. Either way, it has to come out."

"I understand."

Holt took a deep breath and forced a tight smile. "You're quite a lady, whoever you are. Most women—and even men for that matter—would have been completely unnerved by your experience with those Apache. But you look cool and collected."

"Thanks," Jessie said. "But I've gone through this thing before. In Texas, where Ki and I come from, we have our own share of Indian troubles. Mostly Kiowa."

The doctor nodded with understanding. "Now," he said, "if you'd just hold his head steady, let's get this arrow out."

Jessie gripped Gilliam's head and watched as the doctor made two quick incisions out from the arrow's shaft. Bleeding was minimal and Gilliam hardly stirred.

"All right," the doctor said, taking hold of the arrow's shaft with both hands and inhaling deeply. "Here goes."

The doctor pulled, very gently at first, then harder when the arrow resisted his efforts.

"Damn!" Holt swore. "I was afraid of this."

Sweat was beading on his face, so Jessie found a towel and mopped it dry. "So now we try the second plan?"

"No other choice," Holt said. "Let's roll him over on his side and hold him just as still as you can while I make the posterior incision."

Jessie did as she was asked. She was glad that Mrs. Gilliam had fainted and wasn't present, because anyone could see that the arrow was angling downward and that extracting it would mean it would have to be directed even farther down and also bent outward.

For several long minutes, Dr. Holt studied the line of the arrow's shaft, then he would move his finger along the base of Arnold Gilliam's neck. Jessie knew the doctor was trying to project the angle where the arrowhead would emerge.

"All right," the doctor said, "I don't like this and I have to tell you I think I might even inflict lethal damage to his neck but that's a chance that I have to take."

"Then do it," Jessie urged.

The doctor's eyes locked with her own. "Yeah," he whispered, picking up his scalpel again.

His incision was lower than Jessie would have projected and it was deep. As soon as the incision was made, Holt again gripped the arrow's shaft, and this time he began to push downward.

Gilliam moaned and tried to roll his head, but Jessie leaned heavily over the poor man and held her breath.

"It's coming," Holt whispered. "Just a little farther and . . . there it is!"

The bloody arrowhead popped out, and the doctor pushed it on through another two inches and then clipped it off with a pair of heavy shears. As soon as the steel arrowhead dropped, the doctor retracted the shaft, and for the next few minutes, he worked furiously to clean the wound and wrap heavy bandaging tightly around the entire neck to prevent further hemorrhaging.

"Are you all right?" the doctor asked when they were finished.

She picked up the towel and again mopped his face. "Yes. Do you think he'll make it?"

"I do," Holt said. "At least I think he has an excellent chance."

The doctor took the towel from Jessie's hand. "Now," he said, "I'd better take a look at your wound."

"Really, it's just a scratch."

"Please," he said, "I'm a doctor. I'd like to think I should be the judge of what medical attention you may or may not require."

Jessie nodded. She looked toward the door and the doctor seemed to read her thoughts. He went to Ki and explained that he had to examine Jessie's wound and that no one, not even Mrs. Gilliam, should be allowed into the examining room until he was finished.

"Now," the young doctor said, "if you'll just remove that shirt."

"Remove it?" Jessie smiled. "What if I simply pulled it up."

"I'd much prefer you removed it entirely."

Jessie shrugged and slowly unbuttoned her blouse. The young doctor's eyes widened a little when he saw the way her large breasts pushed at their confinement, but he managed to concentrate on the bullet wound.

"Raise your arm and let me have a closer look," the doctor said.

Jessie raised her arm, and when the young doctor placed his hands on her bare stomach, she shivered a little. He gently touched the wound and inadvertently brushed his hands across her breast.

"I'm sorry," he said quickly, looking embarrassed enough to tell Jessie that the move really had been accidental.

"That's all right. Am I going to live?"

"Yes, thank heavens," he told her. "But your corset does create a little problem. You see, I need it out of the way in order to clean the wound and then bandage it."

Jessie raised her eyebrows in question. "And what would you suggest?"

"Undo the corset and . . . well, I suppose just hold it in place."

Jessie tried to reach back around to undo the corset, but the motion hurt and she gasped with pain. "Do you mind, Doctor?"

"Not at all."

34

He untied her corset and it slipped from her breasts. The doctor was standing a little behind her, but Jessie heard him suck in his breath and his fingers froze on her skin.

"Whew," he breathed. "It's getting hotter in here by the minute."

Jessie blushed but let him have his eyeful. She knew that she had the kind of a body that fired a man's blood—even a doctor trying to act professional.

The doctor took his own sweet time cleaning Jessie's wound and then applying a soothing salve. He moved around in front of Jessie, and he was perspiring heavily as he wound another bandage around her ribs.

Dragging his eyes up from her lush breasts only inches from his nose, Dr. Holt said, "I'm afraid I'm going to have to watch this very closely over the next few days. We must not risk the chance of a nasty infection."

Jessie drew her shoulders back a little and smiled to see that her nipples were hardening under his devoted attention.

"No," she said, "we don't want to risk that."

The young doctor gulped and was about to say something when they both heard a woman's voice just outside the door cry, "Arnold! Dear Arnold! I must see my Arnold!"

"Mrs. Gilliam," Jessie said.

The doctor pulled his eyes away from her breasts. "Yes," he said, "I . . . I guess we're done for now."

"For now," Jessie told him. "When will you come and change my bandage?"

Over the loud cries of the woman outside, Dr. Holt said, "I should check up on it as early as tonight—just in case."

"I'll be staying at the Ambassador Hotel," she said with a smile as she pulled on her blouse.

Mrs. Gilliam was a large, highly excitable woman in her early fifties. When Ki finally allowed her entry, she rushed into the examining room, past the doctor and Jessie, and

35

when she saw her husband with his neck completely bound with bandaging, she nearly fainted all over again.

Fortunately, Dr. Holt had anticipated her reaction and had smelling salts handy.

"My God!" the heavyset woman cried. "Will my Arnold live?"

Dr. Holt took Arnold's pulse. "Your husband is a fighter, Mrs. Gilliam. We were able to extract that arrow from his neck without losing too much more blood. I think he's going to be just fine if he gets through the next hour or two."

Mrs. Gilliam burst into tears, and that was when Jessie made her exit. Outside, there was still a large crowd, and Jessie again reiterated how Yuma's own Arnold Gilliam had saved the stagecoach and her life.

And when she and Ki finally managed to break away and head for the Ambassador Hotel, Ki said, "Did he really shoot three Indians?"

"No," Jessie said, "but the only thing that matters is that he and this town *think* he did."

Ki did not ask for an explanation and Jessie did not offer one. All she wanted now was a bath, a meal, and bed—and maybe, for a while, a handsome and very capable young doctor.

★

Chapter 5

That evening, Jessie removed her bandage and took a long, luxuriating bath. Then she ordered a meal brought up to her room. The Ambassador Hotel was good that way; they had an excellent restaurant, and room service was far better than anyone would expect to find in a hot little desert town like Yuma.

The dinner she ordered was baked catfish, caught fresh each day by boys who earned their spending money that way from the hotel and other cafés. Besides the catfish, she had corn bread muffins and coffee.

Dressed in a light wrapper and settled in for the evening, Jessie discovered that she was very hungry and that just sitting stationary after so many long days of stage travel was a blessing.

She finished her meal and was about to spend an hour or so reading over some company reports when there was a knock at her door. It wasn't the samurai, who was resting in the adjoining room, because he had a special knock.

"Who is it?"

"Dr. Holt."

Jessie smiled and went to the door. The doctor handed her a bouquet of flowers and said, "You look too healthy to be anyone's patient."

"Oh, but I'm not," Jessie said, taking his arm and closing the door behind them.

She untied the sash that bound her white satin wrapper and pulled it aside.

"See?"

The doctor gulped, and his eyes drank in the beauty of her lush body. He saw her long, shapely legs, golden-haired honey pot, beautiful hips, and flat tummy. Everything was perfect except the grazed flesh of her bullet wound, to which his medical training forced him to attend.

"Hmmm," he mused. "I had better rebandage that right now."

Jessie thrust her breasts out a little. "It isn't bleeding. Maybe we could wait to do that until you leave. What do you think?"

"Yes," he said with a smile. "Think that's just what the doctor will order."

Holt's long, slender fingers stroked Jessie's flat belly, and she shivered with expectation. His fingers slipped down to her womanhood, and one of them gently explored until it touched the center of her greatest pleasure.

"What are you doing?" she breathed. "Expanding your professional examination?"

He bent his head and began to kiss her breasts. "That's right," he said as his finger slipped into her heat and began to wiggle.

Jessie lifted to him, hips working in an elliptical motion, breath starting to come fast.

"Wouldn't this be easier on the bed?" she suggested.

"Maybe." Dr. Holt unbuttoned his fly and pulled out his thick rod. "But I like to experiment a little."

Jessie groaned. She didn't know what this man had in mind, but she was willing and able to satisfy.

Holt reached around, cupped her firm buttocks in his hands,

and then, baring his teeth and thrusting his rod forward, impaled her where she stood.

"Uggh," Jessie groaned, retreating as the young doctor began to thrust and bump her across the room until she was backed against a wall.

Holt ravaged her breasts with his lips and tongue. He became almost violent as his passion mounted, and Jessie loved it. The picture on the wall nearby began to jump, and then it crashed to the floor, but neither of them cared.

"Oh yes!" Jessie cried, jumping up and wrapping her legs around his hips.

The doctor pumped furiously, and Jessie clung to him as the wall shook, until at last he threw back his head and gasped, filling her with his seed, her own body shuddering powerfully and moaning with relief as she milked the doctor dry.

He carried her over to the bed and they collapsed, both trying to catch their breath.

"My," Jessie said when she could speak. "That *was* different!"

"I wanted to do that the first time I saw you. I wanted it just that way, too." He grinned boyishly. "I never took a woman for the very first time standing."

Jessie chuckled. This doctor was a tiger in the flesh, very unlike his cool professional self when treating a patient.

"Did you like it?" he asked.

"I loved it, but I'd like to try you on this bed the next time."

He was still fully dressed and rolled off her to pull his gold watch from his vest. "I think that should be about fifteen minutes from now."

"That soon?"

"Uh-huh," he said. "And I promise that the second time will be much slower and gentler. I don't normally act like such an animal but you're so beautiful, I knew that I'd have damn little control the first time we made love."

Jessie understood. A lot of men found her so exciting that they came very quickly at first, then later in the same love-making session concentrated on long, long, mutually satisfying copulations.

Dr. Holt stood up and began to undress. "I only have two suits," he explained, "and the other one is at the Chinese laundry up the street being cleaned and pressed. I can't afford to leave here looking as if I've been doing anything improper."

"Of course not," Jessie said. "Though I have the feeling that this is not the first time you've coupled with a patient."

"Of course not!" he said cheerfully as he pulled off his shirt and pants. "But don't get the idea that I prey on my female patients, because that is certainly not the case. It's just that they can be so . . . so grateful for my medical services!"

Jessie had to laugh. "I'm grateful too. But I could have paid you cash."

"There isn't enough money in the world to replace making love to you, Miss Starbuck."

"You are quite a rogue, Dr. Holt. I think you might have to worry about jealous husbands and lovers coming after you."

"I'm very discreet and an excellent marksman besides, though I hope never to take a man's life. After all, I took the Hippocratic oath to preserve life, not expend it."

"Good point," Jessie said. "And speaking of saving lives, how is Arnold Gilliam doing?"

"He's going to be fine," the doctor said. "That arrow that we took from his neck probably missed his jugular by less than a quarter inch and it's quite miraculous that there was no spinal injury. The incident is so extraordinary that I'm going to write it up for submission to a medical journal. I've even arranged for a photographer to take pictures."

"Do you think that Mr. Gilliam would approve?"

"Of course! In fact, when he regained consciousness and

40

his wife finally gained some composure, I put the question to them on the spot." The doctor grinned. "They were, as you might expect, a little shocked, especially when I told them that I wanted to fix the arrow so it appeared to still be protruding from his neck."

Jessie shook her head in amazement. "I can't believe that they agreed."

"Oh, but they did! I promised to pay for the photographer and when I told them that their picture would be in a prestigious medical journal and that they might even be asked to go to Boston for our medical society's annual symposium—all expenses paid—they were most agreeable!"

Jessie laughed. "What a difference this is all making in that little man's life!"

Dr. Holt kicked off his shoes and tore off his socks. He pushed Jessie's legs apart and climbed onto her, his rod hard and thick again.

"I don't even think it's been fifteen minutes yet," she grunted as he drove himself deep into her hot wetness. "I don't think it's been ten minutes yet!"

Holt moaned and opened his eyes. "It will be well past that time when I empty myself into you again, lovely woman."

Jessie clung to the man and let her body respond naturally. In a few minutes, she was moaning and thrashing under his assault and her fingernails were raking the young doctor's back, further firing his passion.

"Doctor," she panted, "you missed your calling."

His handsome face was glistening with perspiration, and the friction of their thrusting bodies was making them slick and causing sucking sounds as their union grew increasingly frantic.

"And what should my true calling have been?" he groaned.

"A gigolo."

He stopped thrusting and looked down at her to say, "Are

41

you offering me a job? I'd come very high, you know."

"You'd be worth it," Jessie breathed, "but I'm going to let Yuma keep you awhile longer."

He laughed with delight and spent the next thirty minutes bringing Jessie's body to a shuddering climax before his back arched and he filled her with his fresh seed.

The doctor left about midnight and Jessie immediately fell into an exhausted sleep that did not end until she was awakened by a familiar knock on her door.

"Be right there, Ki!" she called, pulling on the satin wrapper and rubbing the sleep from her eyes.

On her way to the door, Jessie felt a little soreness between her legs to remind her that she had given and received a lot of pleasure from a real stallion of a man. Dr. Holt's scent was thick in her nostrils, and her face and breasts were sensitive from whisker burn.

When she opened the door, Ki stepped inside and studied her with a cool appraisal. "It's almost noon," he said, "and I thought you might want to get something to eat. The stage for California is leaving about two o'clock."

"Thank you," she said, "I must have been more tired than I thought last night."

The samurai said nothing, but she could tell by his masked expression that she had not fooled him at all. He'd probably heard the walls shaking and then the picture shatter on the floor. If the samurai had thought for a single instant that Jessie was being hurt rather than pleasured, he'd have been at her side in a heartbeat.

"I'll be waiting next door," Ki said.

Jessie nodded and closed her door. She would have liked to have taken a second bath, but there really wasn't time, so she cleaned herself with a washrag and fresh, cool water. She brushed her long, strawberry blond hair until it shone with a luster, then she dressed in her traveling clothes. She was not at all looking forward to this, the final leg of her stagecoach journey to California.

Twenty minutes later, she and the samurai were having a nice lunch in the hotel's excellent restaurant. Each time a new patron appeared, Jessie looked up quickly, hoping it was Dr. Holt and he would join them, but her young lover did not make an appearance.

"We might as well go upstairs and get our things and head for the stageline's office," Jessie said when they were finished eating.

Ki nodded with agreement. Jessie paid and was about to head for the staircase that would take her to her room when she finally saw the young doctor rush into the hotel. His face was grim and set, causing Jessie's smile to fade.

"What's wrong!" she asked, gripping his arm.

"News just came in that the eastbound stage was attacked by Apache and everyone except some half-breed kid was either wounded or killed."

Jessie's hand flew to her mouth. "No!" she whispered, thinking of her dear old family friend, Alton Lamont.

"I'm afraid so," the doctor said. "The details are real sketchy. The stationmaster out there loaded up and pulled out. He said that he wasn't going to be the next one to get shot full of arrows."

"But how does he know who was killed?"

"I can't say," the doctor replied. "The sheriff is trying to form a posse but he's not having any luck. No one wants to go out there while the Apache are on the warpath. Hell, they've attacked three stagecoaches in a row now!"

"Well someone has to go and see if there are any survivors who need help."

"That's right. I'm going and so is the sheriff. But we aren't getting any other volunteers."

"We'll go."

43

"No!" Dr. Holt lowered his voice. "I didn't mean to sound rough, but no. Besides, you've got a stage to California to catch. There are no marauding Indians to the west of us."

"One of the passengers," Jessie said, "was a man named Alton Lamont and he was a dear friend of my father's and also of mine. I couldn't go on to California thinking I might be of service to dear old Lamont."

"Even if I said yes," Holt argued, "I know that Sheriff Benson wouldn't allow you or any other woman to come."

"He really can't stop us." Jessie turned to her samurai as she opened her purse and extracted several hundred dollars. "Ki, I want you to buy whatever we'll need. Horses and saddles, water skins and food for ourselves and the animals. Buy enough to take care of our needs for at least a week."

Ki disappeared, leaving Dr. Holt to shake his head with exasperation. "Listen, Jessie," he said, "the sheriff has to go investigate and there might be wounded people out there somewhere whose lives I can save. But there's *nothing* that you can do and it's foolish to risk your life and that of the samurai for nothing."

"I told you," Jessie said, "Alton Lamont is a dear friend and he might need our help. We're going no matter what you or your sheriff say, so let's stop arguing about this."

"All right." Holt expelled a deep breath. "I'll try to talk the sheriff into agreeing. But it won't be easy."

"Easy or not, he can't stop us from traveling the same road we came into Yuma on," Jessie said. "And if it helps, tell him that we're both seasoned fighters."

"He won't believe that of a woman."

"Tough," Jessie said with rising anger in her voice. "And tell him that Ki is worth any three posse members that he could have recruited in Yuma."

"I won't tell him that," Dr. Holt said. "It would just rile him all the more."

Jessie headed on up the stairs. "I can hardly wait to meet your sheriff," she called down. "He must be a real pigheaded man."

Holt looked up at her, and despite the seriousness of their circumstances, he chuckled and gave her a smile. "Jessie," he said, "you are one hell of a woman."

"Thanks," she called back as she hurried down the hallway to her room, where she would make ready this desperate ride back into the desert hell via the stage station at Gila Crossing.

Thirty minutes later, Jessie and Ki were mounted and riding their horses up the street to meet Dr. Holt and the sheriff. There was a large crowd gathered in the street, and a lot of anxious-looking men were arguing.

"Excuse me," Jessie said, reining her horse through the crowd. "Sheriff, are your ready?"

He was a big man, beefy-faced and slope-shouldered. He wore a long, pale mustache that was waxed at the tips and reminded Jessie of the horns of a Texas longhorn bull.

"You and that Chinaman sure as hell ain't going!" Sheriff Benson shouted.

"Maybe not with you and the doctor," Jessie shouted right back, "but we're going."

"The hell you say!"

Jessie reined her horse, a fine buckskin, away, saying, "We don't need them, Ki. And we don't need this excuse for a lawman giving us a hard time."

"Hey!" the sheriff raged. "Where are you two going!"

"Gila Crossing!"

"You can't do that!"

In answer, Jessie gave the buckskin a touch of her boot heels, and the mare went into a gallop that carried her swiftly out of Yuma, heading east. The samurai was right beside her, riding stirrup to stirrup.

About a mile east of town, Jessie twisted around in her saddle to see Sheriff Benson and Dr. Holt come flying out of Yuma in their wake.

The samurai also twisted around. "The sheriff is going to make this difficult, Jessie."

"I know. Can't be helped. It's a free country and this is a free road. We're going to find out what happened to our friend, sheriff be damned."

"And if he tries to stop us?"

"Use *atemi* on him," Jessie said. *Atemi* was the samurai word for applying pressure to some point in such a forceful manner that the victim lost consciousness—for a few minutes, up to more than an hour, depending on the samurai's wishes.

"For how long?"

Jessie thought about it for a minute or two before she said, "Put Sheriff Benson out for as long as you can. That ought to impress Dr. Holt."

The samurai nodded. All he had to do was to get within reach of Sheriff Benson and his orders were as good as done. It would be better this way anyhow. The samurai did not think that Sheriff Benson was the kind of man with whom it would be pleasant to ride a long, hot desert trail.

★

Chapter 6

Jessie let the sheriff chase them for about two miles and then she signaled Ki that it was time to rein in and have their little showdown.

By the time that Sheriff Benson and Dr. Holt overtook them, the lawman was so angry that he appeared ready to have an attack of apoplexy.

"Godammit!" he bellowed, dragging his horse to a stop. "I told you both to stay in Yuma! I got enough to worry about without having to nursemaid a couple of greenhorns."

Dr. Holt tried to reason with the sheriff. "I don't think they're greenhorns," he said. "After all, they're the ones that helped Mr. Gilliam bring that stage into town."

"I don't give a damn! They won't be so lucky a second time."

"Luck," Jessie said, "hasn't a thing to do with it. And besides, one of the men on the stage is a friend and I mean to find out if he can be helped."

"The only help you'll be," the sheriff said, "is to keep your pretty ass in Yuma!"

Jessie's cheeks flamed. It was clear now that the sheriff of Yuma was not a reasonable man. There was little point in carrying on this discussion a moment longer. She nodded to the samurai.

Ki took the signal and reined his horse in toward Sheriff Benson, who went for his six-gun.

"You're under arrest, by—"

The lawman never had time to finish. Ki's arm shot out, and his thumb and forefinger pinched into a very specific place on the sheriff's neck. The big man's eyes bulged, and he almost got his gun out of his holster before he toppled from his horse to land heavily on the dirt road.

"What the hell did you do to him!" Holt cried, jumping from his horse to kneel by the sheriff's side.

"As you can plainly see," Jessie said, "the sheriff hasn't suffered any permanent harm. Ki simply halted the flow of blood to his brain and he fainted. I promise you that he'll be just fine in an hour or so."

Dr. Holt looked up at the samurai. "In medical school we learned where the pressure points were, but I never saw or believed anyone could find and apply them so dramatically."

"A samurai calls it *atemi*."

The doctor took the sheriff's pulse and then thumbed up his eyelids. "An hour, you say?"

"About," Ki answered.

"So what do we do with him now?"

Jessie shrugged her shoulders. "We leave him here and go on, of course. When he awakens, he can either return to Yuma—"

"He won't do that," Holt interrupted. "How would he explain it to everyone?"

"Then let him follow us," Jessie said. "If he would only be reasonable, we could sure use his gun in case we are jumped by the Apache."

Holt nodded. He climbed back into his saddle. "I hate to leave him like this. If an Apache came along and found him . . ."

48

"They won't," Ki said. "It would be stupid for the Apache to come this close to Yuma."

Holt did not appear entirely convinced, but he nodded his head and followed Jessie and Ki as they continued down the road.

Late that afternoon, they saw smoke on the eastern horizon and pulled their horses to a halt.

"That would be just about where we'll find the Gila Crossing station," Ki said.

Jessie nodded with agreement. "I'm afraid that we might be too late to help anyone," she said. "Let's go real slow and be careful. We might be riding into more trouble than we can handle."

Dr. Holt swallowed nervously, and seeing the perspiration that bathed his face, Jessie said, "You can go back if you want. No one will blame you, least of all me."

"No," he said, "I'm sticking."

"Good." Jessie was proud of the doctor. It was clear to her that he was not a man accustomed to riding into the desert and facing Apache, but he was game and he wasn't going to back down out of fear.

About a mile from the station, Ki kicked his horse into a trot and went on ahead. The samurai rode to a small rise of land and they could see him dismount, then tie his horse to a bit of brush before he crept up to the rise. He flattened and lay still, eyes just above the apex of the rise.

"What do you think?" Holt asked.

"I don't know," Jessie said. "I expect that we'll find out soon enough."

Holt nodded his head in agreement, and when the samurai came to his feet and waved them to come on ahead, the young doctor sighed with relief. A few minutes later, Jessie and the doctor joined Ki at the crown of the rise.

"Holy mackerel!" the doctor said when he saw the smoking

ruins below and three dead horses lying in the yard. "It looks as if they had quite a battle."

"And the Apache won," Jessie said in a grim tone of voice. "Let's go see what we can find out."

All three of them were tight as coiled springs as they rode slowly down toward what was left of the stage station. Jessie held her saddle rifle in her fists, and the samurai had his bow fitted with an arrow. The doctor had left Yuma in such a hurry that he'd forgotten to bring a saddle rifle, and all he had was a Colt revolver.

Their mounts spooked at the dead horses, and about twenty yards away, Jessie saw the body of one of the stage hostlers. It was pincushioned with arrows and there was a large black patch where the man had been scalped. The air was filled with flies and the stench of death.

Jessie dismounted and the two men at her sides did the same. She stood motionless for several moments and looked to the samurai, whose instincts were very keen.

"What do you think?"

"Probably everyone here is dead."

"There's only one way to find out," Jessie said. "Let's go slow and look sharp. Sometimes people can survive when you least expect."

"In this carnage?" the doctor said. "Not a chance."

But five minutes later, they discovered that one of the stage employees had somehow managed to escape the station and hide in the brush. He had taken at least three bullets, and when they found him, he was nearly crazy with thirst.

"Get some water for him," Jessie said urgently as she knelt by his side and cradled his head while Dr. Holt tore open the man's shirt and examined the wounds.

Jessie saw that one bullet had traveled through the man's chest and that another had penetrated his abdomen, while the last had shattered his upper arm. She could not imagine the pain he must be suffering.

"Doc Holt!"

"Yes," the doctor said, "do you know me?"

"Seen you patch up a few in Yuma," the man said through clenched teeth. "Have I bought it?"

The doctor sighed. "I'm afraid that you have."

The dying man was perhaps forty years old, dirty, unkempt, and unshaven. His eyes were glazed with pain but showed no fear, only suffering.

"You got any whiskey or anything that'd help me?" the man asked. "I'm dyin' hard, Doc. It's worse than I ever figured it'd be."

"My medical kit is tied to my horse. I've got some laudanum. It'll kill the pain."

"But no whiskey?"

"I'm sorry."

The man's smile was painful to watch. "That's all right, Doc. But I would have liked to have one more drink. Ain't had a drink in two years, you understand. Whiskey was my downfall. That's why I stayed out here in this hellish place. Wasn't easy to get something to drink. But now . . . now that I'm buyin' it, I'd like to get drunk once more."

"I've got some whiskey in my saddlebags," Jessie said to the doctor. "Bring it back with you."

Holt nodded and moved off. Jessie saw the samurai searching just in case anyone else might have made it out of the burning stage station alive.

"What happened?" Jessie asked the man. "We need to know."

He sniffled. "Ain't much to tell. They hit us right at dawn. Came in from all sides. Me and two others went down before we even had a chance to get back into the station. I crawled off into the brush but not before I was shot twice more. Then

51

things got so busy that the Apache forgot about me. They were trying to set the station on fire."

"They succeeded."

The man gulped. "Yeah, but not before they lost a few of their own. I crawled out here and lay all morning listening to the fight. Then, when I smelled the smoke, I started to hear men screaming. There was a lot of shooting and I guess that they tried to escape the station and were shot down."

"Did you see anything?"

The man squeezed his eyes shut very tightly. "I was too scared to see much of anything. I heard that tall old man yelling for his half-breed."

"What!"

"That's right. The eastbound stage was attacked the night before. Only ones that survived were that old man and the half-breed kid. Somehow, they made it here to Gila Crossing and we was all plannin' to get the hell on to Yuma when the Apache came again early this morning."

"You say that Mr. Lamont died?"

"I can't say. I heard the kid yelling and then I must have passed out. God, I need somethin' for this pain!"

"The doctor is coming," Jessie said just as Holt arrived.

"Here's the laudanum and—"

"To hell with it!" the dying man croaked, reaching for Jessie's bottle of expensive whiskey. "This is what I want to die of!"

"You guzzle that bottle down," the doctor said, "and it'll kill you within a few minutes."

"Good!"

They both watched as the man upended the bottle and began to pour the whiskey down his gullet, choking and spitting.

When the bottle was gone, the man closed his eyes with a sigh and panted, "I thank you very much. I forgot how good whiskey tastes. I should have stayed in Yuma and drank myself to death. Anything would have been better than goin' this way."

Jessie couldn't argue with the man. She looked at the doctor, and then Ki came over to join them.

"There're no others. Looks like the Apache must have thrown all the bodies into the flames before they took what stage horses they could find and rode away."

"How long ago?"

"Three, four hours." Ki paused a minute. "I have something else you're going to find very interesting. I think the Apache might have taken a few captives."

"What gives you that idea?"

"I remember the Apache kid was wearing boots without any heels. He'd ripped them off. Sometimes Indians will do that to make walking easier. I found those tracks where he mounted a horse and rode away."

Jessie remembered that there had been talk of the half-breed and how he'd survived. She did not know how that rumor started, but now she had to admit that it just might have some basis in fact.

"Ki," she said. "If Juara went with them, perhaps he was able to spare Mr. Lamont. He'd try and protect him."

"I found bootprints," Ki said, "so that's possible."

"That's fantasy!" Holt exclaimed. "What you probably found were the tracks of an Apache that was wearing boots he took off of one of the dead before he threw the man into the flames."

"Maybe," Jessie said stubbornly, "but we don't know that for certain. It *could* be Mr. Lamont!"

"Why would the Apache save him?"

Jessie thought about it for a moment. "Lamont is very rich. It's conceivable that Juara could have spared his life by promising that Lamont would buy them guns or give them a huge sum of money. Something like that."

"Oh, come on now! That doesn't make sense."

53

"Yes, it does," Jessie said. "The Apache trade with Comancheros and others for weapons, ammunition, food, and whiskey. That takes money or stolen goods. The Apache might not have understood the importance of a white man's gold or money ten years ago, but that's all changed now."

Jessie looked to Ki. "We've got to go after them and find out if Lamont and the boy are being held hostage."

"You're both mad!" Holt exclaimed.

Just then, the man whose head Jessie cradled gave a long sigh and breathed his last. Jessie stood up.

"Let's find something to dig with and bury him and that other poor man we saw out in the brush. Then let's follow the Apache tracks until we know for sure whether or not Mr. Lamont is alive."

Ki dipped his chin in agreement and then left to search for a shovel or some other digging tool.

"I can't believe I'm hearing you correctly," Holt said. "Have you contracted sunstroke?"

"No," Jessie told the man. "But we came out here to find out what happened to them, and we still don't know. Ki and I are not leaving until the mystery is solved."

"You'll get killed for sure," Dr. Holt said.

"Don't bet your shingle on that, Doctor," Jessie warned before she went off to help Ki search for a shovel or a pick.

"I can't let you go off and do this alone," Holt said. "I couldn't live with myself if I did that."

Jessie stopped and turned to face the man. "Doctor," she said, touching his cheek, "you'll save hundreds of lives during your medical career. You're needed in Yuma, not out in this desert with us."

"But . . ."

"Please," she said, "Ki and I know what we are undertaking. We're not foolish or rash. We won't take unnecessary chances and we will survive."

Dr. Holt looked deeply into her green eyes. "My head tells me that you're right. That I might even be a detriment to you on the Apache's trail. But my heart . . ."

Jessie touched his lips and smiled. "Last night, we listened to our hearts. Now it's time to listen to our heads. Go back to Yuma."

Holt was about to say something when Ki shouted, "Jessie, over here!"

Jessie turned and hurried over to see what the samurai had found, and Dr. Holt was right on her heels.

"What is it!" Jessie called, coming to a halt next to the samurai.

"Look," Ki said, handing her a crumpled piece of paper.

It was a letter, but almost illegible, the scrawling was so bad. "It's from Mr. Lamont!" Jessie said, sitting right down on the ground and smoothing the paper across her lap.

Jessie leaned forward and slowly began to read out loud. "Juara and I are being taken away by the Indians. Don't know what will happen. Odds not good but contact next of kin not to bury me yet. Alton Lamont."

"Good Lord!" Holt whispered. "That dying man was right!"

Jessie nodded. "Let's get the dead buried and then let's go find Lamont and his young half-breed friend."

Ki pointed toward the south. "They're heading for Old Mexico."

"Then we are too," Jessie said with a look of grim determination.

Chapter 7

Jessie, Ki, and the doctor filled their canteens and water skins, then headed headed straight south across the Sonoran Desert. The Apache's trail was easy to follow because the Indians did not expect pursuit.

Late that first afternoon, Jessie and Ki came upon the half-eaten carcass of a dead horse. The beast had been quartered and its haunches thrown into a fire. Now, the fire was dead and flies swarmed over the remains.

"They don't exactly dine elegantly, do they?" Holt said with a shake of his head.

"They're a hard people," Ki said. "They have to be in order to survive in this kind of hellish country."

"Yeah, I suppose you're right."

Ki dismounted and handed his reins to Jessie. The samurai went to the camp fire and then began to circle around and around, reading tracks. Jessie and Holt watched in silence. The heat and earlier digging of graves had greatly sapped their strength. Their horses were sucked up in the belly from lack of food and water, and already things were grim.

"What did you find?" Jessie asked when the samurai rejoined them.

"They are both still alive," Ki reported. "But Mr. Lamont

is dragging one foot a little. My guess is that he's been wounded."

Jessie shook her head. The old man was not strong enough to take days of hard riding in the heat of the desert. Especially if he was wounded. "Let's keep on riding. We've got another hour of daylight and then we'll ride on until midnight."

The two men reined their horses after her and they kept riding south. It was nearly ten o'clock that night when they came upon a big water spring. It was sitting in a huge sandy basin, and the overflow trickled off into the desert a few hundred yards and then was swallowed up by the hot sands.

Had they not been following the Apache tracks, they could have passed within a hundred yards south of this life-giving water and never even realized it was present.

Their horses were almost unmanageable as they rushed to quench their thirst, and Jessie did not even attempt to slow the animals down. They let them step right into the basin of warmish water and drink their fill.

"Let's spend the night here," Jessie said, reading the tracks in the moonlight and seeing how the Apache had also spent time here filling their water skins.

"I'll sleep up on that low ridge," Ki said, leaving his horse but gathering his weapons and belongings and preparing to hide off in the moonlight.

"You don't need to do that," Holt said. "I mean . . ."

"Never mind what he means," Jessie said, noting the doctor's embarrassment. "We'll sleep easier if we spread out a little. You never know what might show up at a rare desert spring big as this one."

Jessie bid each of the men good night and carried her own saddle and bedroll up near some brush. From hard experience, she and Ki had both learned better than to sleep out in the open when you were in hostile country.

"Good night," Holt called softly.

"Good night," Jessie replied, looking up at a big wedge of golden moon. Her body was exhausted, but her mind would not rest. Jessie thought about Lamont and that reminded her of her late father, Alex Starbuck. Alex had started his career in San Francisco, where he opened a small shop that sold secondhand merchandise and a few objects imported from the Far East.

In a few years, the import business grew to include several waterfront warehouses, and then Alex bought his first sailing ship to bring goods, primarily from Japan and China, directly to his warehouses. Business was so good that he soon added a second ship and then a third. Within four years of opening his little shop, he was well on the way to making his first million dollars. The two ships grew into a fleet of merchant freighters that began to handle not only Alex's business, but that of other West Coast importers as well.

Jessie had been small then, but she vividly remembered the day that her father first took her down to the shipyards and proudly showed her the new iron-hulled steamers that he was sure would be the future of oceanic trade.

"One day," he promised, "I'll have an entire fleet of steam-powered ships and no longer will we have to depend upon the capricious trade winds. We'll collect treasures and products from all over the world!"

Alex's prediction proved to be true. Within another five years, not only had he built a large fleet of steamers, but he'd purchased his own steel mill and enough mines to supply the mill with ores. And by the time that railroad building had started to forever change the face of the West, Alex was also heavily invested in railroad stock. Like everything else he touched, these investments were enormously profitable, and he funneled the profits directly into banks, brokerage houses, and then foreign companies involved in rubber, coffee, and sugar plantations. Before his death, Alex Starbuck had also invested in huge cattle ranches all over the world, but his

58

home and favorite remained the Circle Star in Texas. When he was finally assassinated, Alex had been well on his way to becoming the richest man in America.

Jessie gazed up at the stars and thought about her father and about all his grand ambitions, which made her own seem small and almost insignificant by comparison. True, she had increased the net worth of the Starbuck empire, and she regularly traveled the world overseeing her far-flung operations. But her real love was the West, and she was never more content than when on horseback, wearing tight-fitting jeans and a battered Stetson. Funny, because as worldly as Alex had been, he'd felt the same way.

"Jessie?"

She started, then turned to see Dr. Holt coming over to her side.

"I'm going to sleep," she told him bluntly. "We've had a hard day and tomorrow will probably be worse."

"I know that," he said. "But do you mind if I sleep beside you?"

"Only if you promise to sleep," she told him in a voice that left no questions between them.

"Tell me," he said, smoothing out his bedroll and flopping down on top of it to cradle his head on laced fingers, "what will we do when we find them—if we find them?"

"I don't know," she admitted. "I guess that Ki will help free Mr. Lamont and Juara. After that, we'll be plenty busy just trying to escape with our scalps."

The young doctor said nothing.

"You should have gone back to Yuma after we buried the dead at Gila Crossing."

"Probably," he admitted. "But my pride wouldn't allow that. I just felt that I might be the difference between your living, or dying."

Jessie was touched by this revelation. She reached out and

59

took his hand. "Go to sleep, Doctor. Maybe tomorrow we'll overtake the Apache and things will work out just fine."

"I don't believe that for a single minute," he told her, "but you're right about needing sleep. Good night."

"Good night," Jessie said, closing her eyes and willing herself to drift off to sleep.

Ki awakened them about two hours before dawn. They did not speak or cook a breakfast but quickly saddled their horses and headed south again. By noon, the temperature was searing their lungs and Jessie was almost getting dizzy.

"It has to be ten degrees hotter than yesterday," she said as they pushed slowly on. "Ki?"

He turned.

"Do you think we are in Old Mexico yet?"

"Yes. And I thought that I smelled smoke a few minutes ago."

Holt looked at Jessie. Then he said, "Apache?"

"I don't know," Ki said, "but when we top that low hill just ahead, I think we might see them."

When they were near the crest of the hill, all three of them dismounted and tied their horses, then crept up to have a look down below.

Jessie's heart sank. What they saw was a large agricultural valley fed by a small river. And in its center was the smoking ruins of what had been a Mexican village. They could all see bodies of dead men lying around the plaza. Old women and children were weeping, and here and there older children were trying to dig graves.

"Those Apache seem to leave a trail of death and destruction everywhere they go," the doctor whispered.

Jessie climbed to her feet and brushed the dirt from her clothes. "Let's go down and do what we can for those poor people," she said.

They remounted and rode down into the valley, marveling at the neatness of the fields and seeing how much of the corn had been trampled and taken by the marauding Indians. At their appearance, a boy of about fourteen cried out in alarm, then ran into a shack and reemerged with an old Spanish musket that looked as if it would explode in his hands if fired.

Jessie and Ki both spoke Spanish, and she said, "We come in peace to help you. Don't shoot."

The boy lowered the old musket. His face was dusty and streaked with dried tears. "You come too late to help," he said, noting their rifles and guns. "The murdering Apache have come and taken our corn and a few of our women. They killed my father and my mother is brokenhearted. There is nothing you can do now. Go away and leave us to mourn."

"No," Jessie said, dismounting. "Maybe we can help."

"How?"

She turned to Dr. Holt. "This man is an American doctor. He can help save lives and heal the wounded."

At this, an old man who had been hiding behind the hut stepped out. "You are welcome in our village. But we have lost everything and have nothing to pay for help."

"We don't want anything," Jessie said.

"That's right," Holt said, untying his medical kit and dismounting to attend an old woman whose hand was wrapped with a blood-soaked bandage.

"We can't leave these people until we've helped to bury their dead and attend them," Jessie said to the samurai.

Ki did not need to be told what was required. He first watered their horses, then used his knife to cut them a big feed of corn. Afterward, he found a crude iron shovel and went to help with the burying of the dead.

It was late evening when he saw the young Mexican woman come staggering out of the cornfield. He saw her collapse and then try to rise and continue on into the village.

61

Ki dropped the shovel and hurried to her side. The woman was in terrible shape. Her face was battered and one of her eyes was swollen completely shut. Her lips were thick and clotted with blood, and her long black hair was tangled and matted. Ki judged her to be in her early twenties, and once she had probably been pretty, but now she was not. It was obvious that she had been beaten and raped by the Apache. She'd no doubt been thrown across a horse and taken away to be an Apache slave, but somehow, she'd escaped.

Ki picked her up and carried her into the village. At the sight of the girl, grateful cries went up among the old women, who rushed to her, speaking rapidly in their guttural Spanish.

"Doc," Ki said, "you'd better take a look at this girl. I think she might be injured internally."

Holt pushed aside the old women. He took the girl's pulse and looked at her dilated pupils, then said, "Let's bring her into one of these adobe shacks where I can examine her in private. Her face has no color at all. She may be bleeding inside. It's a wonder to me that she's still alive."

The old Mexican women were not pleased. They yelled in anger, but when Ki and the doctor allowed one to join them inside the nearest hut, they quieted.

"You stay out of his way," Ki warned the old woman. "He is good medicine and you cannot interfere."

The old woman crouched in a corner of the small adobe. There was little furniture save a crude table and several chairs. The beds were simply corn-husk–filled mattresses piled on the floor.

When Holt started to remove the girl's simple peasant dress in order to examine her, the old woman drew a knife from her dress and jumped at the doctor. Had the crone been just a few years younger, Ki might not have been able to save the doctor's life. As it was, he grabbed the old woman's wrist, and with his free hand he applied *atemi*.

The woman crumpled without a sound and Ki tossed her knife under the table.

When the doctor had finished his examination, he carried the girl to a mattress and laid her down, then covered her with a serape.

"I can't do anything for her," Holt said. "If she's bleeding inside, all we can do is hope that it isn't serious and that the bleeding will stop. She's been terribly abused."

Ki studied the girl and felt anger building in his belly. Damn those Apache! The doctor looked over at the old woman. "Maybe you ought to stay with these two until one of them comes around again," Ki said.

"Tell Jessie I'm here."

"I will," Ki promised.

Outside, Ki found Jessie ministering to an old woman who had been struck in the head. There was blood coming out of her ears and she looked dazed and was incoherent. When she saw the samurai and the woven leather band that he wore around his head, she screamed and covered her eyes.

Jessie hugged the old woman, told her that everything was going to be all right.

"But it won't be," she told Ki in English. "The Apache have killed off all but the very young and very old men. From what I can gather, they keep just enough alive to plant, tend, and harvest these cornfields."

Ki understood. These poor village people were little more than a colony of half-starved slaves who spent their lives working to satisfy the fierce Apache.

"We need to end this," Ki said. "They fear me but they will talk to you. Ask them how soon they believe the Apache will return."

Jessie nodded and asked. She did not have to translate to the samurai. He understood perfectly well. The Apache would come often during the harvest to collect more corn.

"Ask her how many and if she saw your friend Lamont with them."

"I already did," Jessie said. "And no, this bunch is not the same that attacked the stage. But sometimes they join up and raid to the north."

"So how many can we expect back here?"

"Twenty or more."

Ki frowned, then studied the village's misery. He did not know how they could defeat so many Apache when they returned, but he figured he'd find some way.

Jessie seemed to read his mind. "When these people calm down a little, we can talk to them. Maybe there are a few that are capable of holding and firing a gun."

"They'd only waste good ammunition," Ki said.

"Then what can we do?" Jessie asked. "There are only three of us."

"It will be enough if we set a trap for them when they come," Ki said.

"What kind of trap?"

"I don't know yet," Ki admitted, "but between us, we will think of something."

Jessie also looked around at the smoking ruins and the trampled cornfields. She saw old women and little children weeping over the bodies of their husbands and fathers.

"Yes," Jessie said through clenched teeth. "By the time those murderers return, we will have thought of something all right."

Chapter 8

The next day was filled with grief. Since the village was too small to warrant a priest, the deceased were buried without benefit of a funeral Mass.

"It seems almost as if they accept death as the price they must pay to live in this hard land," Jessie said, watching the villagers as they prayed and mourned their dead.

"It's probably all they've ever known," Holt said.

Ki agreed. "We must change that. No one should have to live this way."

"I'll do what I can to save the injured," the doctor said, "but some of the men have terrible wounds. I'm afraid that more will die."

"I'll help you tend to their needs," Jessie offered.

That evening, Ki finished helping fill in the last grave, and then, with darkness falling softly across the little agricultural valley, he walked out into the hills and sat down to study the land. He was seeking some way in which the village below might be defended against the cruel Apache, who had probably been inflicting death and starvation upon these peasants for many generations. It amazed Ki that the villagers did not simply pack up and leave, but he knew that they were tied to this rich farmland. And where would they go anyway? Down to the great Mexico City? Or to another village where they would be landless strangers?

Even as Ki was thinking of the people down below, one of them left the village and came walking across the fields toward him. The samurai waited quietly in the moonlight, and it was only when the figure drew within a few yards that he called out in Spanish, "Who are you?"

"Conchita," she replied.

Ki frowned. It was the girl he had found and carried into the village. She should be resting and recovering instead of walking out into the night.

"What do you want?"

She did not answer until she stood before him. "I have been watching you," she said with simple directness. "I want to know where you come from."

"Texas. Have you heard of it?"

The girl nodded. "What are you? You do not look like anyone I know."

"At least you do not judge me as a Chinaman."

"Señor?"

"Never mind. I am from another land far away across the oceans."

"Oceans?"

"Great waters," he told her, realizing that he should not be surprised that a simple peasant girl might have trouble imagining oceans. After all, she had probably never been farther than ten miles from this village until the Apache carried her away.

"How old are you?" he asked.

"Nineteen."

"Has no one told you that there are other worlds?"

"This *is* my world," she said. "I had a husband, but the Apache killed him last year. I hope to have another husband some day so that I might have children."

66

Ki looked sideways at her in the moonlight. "An Apache warrior would have taken you to wife."

Conchita spit on the ground. "They are animals! I would kill them all if I could!"

She took a seat beside the samurai. "But I do not think that I will find another husband. All the young men are dead. The old ones are too old to father children."

Ki nodded with understanding. This peasant girl's frank conversation did not embarrass him in the least. Quite the contrary because he appreciated her candor. And although he had visited Mexico with Jessie on several occasions, this was really the first time he'd ever had a girl talk to him from her heart.

"Señor Ki, you are a very brave man to stay here with us. And the señorita with the light hair, she is beautiful, no?"

"Yes, very."

Conchita leaned a little closer. "She is your woman, no?"

"No."

Conchita frowned, a question in her black eyes. "She does not want so brave a man as you?"

Ki had to smile. "It is not that."

"What then?"

"It's just that she and I are friends."

"Oh," Conchita said as though that made sense to her. "Will she have your children then?"

"No." Ki expelled a deep breath. He could, he knew, simply tell this woman-child that it was none of her business and that he wished her to go back to the village so that he could think about how he might defend it when the Apache returned. That would have been the easiest thing to do, but Ki found he liked the smell and the feel of her presence. Considering the ordeal she had just suffered, it was remarkable that she did not hate all men.

"Listen," he said patiently, "I work for Señorita Starbuck."

"You work for her?"

"I am samurai," Ki said, "and I have sworn to protect her from harm."

"If the Apache catch her, they will harm her plenty. You should run, Señor Ki. They will kill you slow."

"I am sure that they will try," he said. "But a samurai is not the easiest person to kill and—"

"Do you have a woman?"

"Now what has that got to do with what we were talking about?" he asked.

"I do not care about this samurai you speak of," she told him. "I need a man now so that the seed of the Apache in me is washed away."

"What are you talking about?"

Her face twisted with hatred. "I hate the Apache! If I found myself in child by them, I might kill myself and be damned to hell."

"Is that what this conversation is all about? That you're afraid that the Apache have gotten you with child?"

Conchita nodded. "I would rather be dead."

Ki could see that she was serious. Furthermore, he saw that her eyes were wet with tears. "Conchita," he said gently, "you must not talk in such a way. If you were with Apache child, it would not be a sin against you or the child."

"They would know and they would take it away someday and it would return to kill the people of my village," she told him with simple conviction. "And *that* would be my curse."

Ki scrubbed his face and tried to think of how he could reason with this girl. The truth of the matter was, he could not reason with her at all. She was simple, childlike, and utterly convinced that she would kill herself if she became pregnant with a renegade Apache's child.

"Señor Ki," she said, "you helped me before. Please help me now."

"By . . . ?"

She laid her hand on his thigh. "I have watched you all day and I see that your manhood is strong. Stronger even than that of an Apache. Before they all come and torture you to death, you must leave something of yourself in me. Something to wash away their seed."

"This is crazy talk."

"You do not understand things like this," she explained. "But a woman can tell. If you do not do this, I will be with Apache child. If you had not found me, then this curse would not be upon me now. Therefore, señor, you are also to blame."

Ki shook his head. He had had many women in his time, but this beat everything. He was not even sure that he could make love to this poor ignorant girl, given her reasoning.

Her hand slipped down his leg and rested on his crotch. She said, "I would not ask this except that you saved my life before. Now you must do it again."

"By breeding you?"

"Yes."

Ki laid back against the side of the hill and looked up at the stars. He did not like the idea of being used; nor did he want to father a child. He seriously doubted that a woman could tell she had been impregnated at conception, and yet . . . yet he knew that there were many mysteries about the opposite sex that he would never understand.

While he was thinking about what to tell this girl, she slipped her hand under his waistband and found his manhood. And just when Ki was deciding that he wanted to be no part of this craziness, she went and pulled his trousers down and took him in her mouth.

Just that quick, all his objections vanished like smoke in the wind. Ki sighed with pleasure as Conchita's lips and tongue worked up and down his stiffening shaft. A smile formed on

69

his lips as she sucked noisily on his root and brought it up as straight as a flagpole.

She lifted her head, lips glistening. "Señor Ki?"

"Yeah?"

"You are much man, no?"

"Whatever you say."

She giggled and went back down on him, her hot mouth doing fantastic things until his hips began to move and he felt a deep, throbbing ache fill his sack.

"You'd better not wait too much longer if you want me to wash away the Apaches' seed," he growled.

Conchita ran her tongue around the head of his big root; then she stood up and slipped out of the simple peasant dress she wore. At the sight of her body, bruised but washed earlier in the river below, Ki felt a mixture of tenderness and passion. In her he saw strength, simplicity, and an illogical faith in her own beliefs. And he saw a woman grinning with satisfaction as she hunched her bottom down to impale herself on his slick root.

"Ahh!"

Ki would have pulled out of Conchita had he been on top, but he wasn't, and she locked her thighs around his hips and pushed past her pain to bury his manhood deep inside.

"You put it in deep," she breathed, "deeper than any damned Apache!"

The samurai understood and nodded his assent. He grabbed her by the buttocks and rolled her over, then slammed his rod even farther up into her bruised but eager body.

Conchita responded powerfully. She thrust herself upward so hard that Ki was afraid he would drive his manhood into her belly. He tried to pull back a little, but she wrapped her legs around his back and milked him wildly.

"All right," he grunted as the last of his resolve melted into passion, "take it deep!"

Conchita sank her teeth into his shoulder and drew blood, but Ki did not even feel pain because every fiber of his body was aflame as his lean, powerful hips pistoned in and out of the Mexican girl until she was screaming under him and his loins emptied into her womb.

She fainted. It had never happened before to the samurai. He froze, feeling his rod still pulsing hugely.

"Conchita!"

She blinked and was back again almost as quickly as she'd gone. Crying and laughing, she clutched his body with gratitude.

"Thank you, Señor Ki! Thank you!"

He raised his head and looked down at her poor swollen face. "Any time, señorita. Any time at all."

Conchita hugged his neck. "We must do this all night to make sure. Please?"

"Are you sure? You've been through a lot. I don't want to hurt you inside."

"You make me well again," she told him. "You do me great honor to have your child."

The samurai wiped away her tears and marveled at her faith and her strength. He had no idea how many Apache had raped her, but it might have been a crowd and it might have been all of them several times. And yet, here she was, convinced that his seed alone would join her seed to create a child that she could love and admire.

"Conchita," he said, "I find you to be very good. I admire you more than the most worldly woman I have had. Far, far more."

"For as long as you stay, you are my man," she told him. "And I will fight the Apache to the death to save your life."

He believed her. And in believing, Ki knew that he *had* to find some way to save this village and these simple, honest Mexican people.

71

★

Chapter 9

"Without guns and rifles," Jessie said one afternoon as they sat in the shade of an adobe shack, "these people haven't a chance of repelling the Apache raiders."

"I know," Ki said. "For a while, I thought that I might be able to show them how to use *te*, the art of hand fighting. But it is clear to me now that these people are too frightened to fight the Indians with their bare hands."

Dr. Holt agreed. "Just the mention of the Apache starts their pulses to racing. But who can blame them for their fears? Women raped, men shot down, crops stripped from their fields. I don't know how these people can exist."

"They've been existing under the rule of the Apache for so many years that they don't know anything better," Ki said. "When you've spent your entire life with something, you can't imagine what living well even means."

"Which brings us full circle to the question that I've been worrying about," Jessie said. "If these villagers are willing to accept this life, do you really believe they would fight the Apache—even if we armed and trained them?"

"I don't know," Ki admitted. "But I think they would. The older boys realize that they'll be slaughtered as soon as they reach manhood. They'd fight."

"But you're talking about fourteen- and fifteen-year-old boys!" Holt argued. "How can they possibly stand up to Apache warriors?"

"They will if they're shown what to do, because they know they have to either fight, or die. They've seen what's happened to their fathers, older brothers, uncles, and cousins. I've talked to many of them and they swear they won't run if they have any chance at all."

"The young women will fight as well," Jessie said. "I've spoken to them. They say they'd rather die than be raped and abducted by the Apache, than made to bear their children." She took a breath. "Then that's it," she said. "Where can I buy weapons for these people?"

"I am told that there is a Mexican garrison to the south," Ki said. "They would have rifles and ammunition."

"If so," Holt said angrily, "why don't they use them to protect their citizens?"

"I don't know," Ki said. "But my experience is that Mexican soldiers, from officer to the lowest infantryman, are not well paid or provisioned and are rarely motivated to glory."

"True," Jessie said. "The Mexican Army often conscripts its soldiers out of the poorest villages and pays them little or nothing. Sometimes, they are not even properly fed or clothed."

"Would they sell weapons to us?" Holt asked.

"Yes," Jessie answered, "for the right price, they would probably sell their souls."

It was a harsh assessment, yet Ki knew that it was true. He and Jessie had had more than one run-in with the Mexican Army and the experience had never been pleasant.

"All right then," the doctor said. "What about money? They'll want pesos and—"

"They'll want dollars even more," Jessie said. "And I just happen to have a few stashed away."

"Who will go?"

Jessie studied the village. "I'd better go."

Ki objected. "Please," he said, "it will be dangerous traveling in this country. Let me go."

"No," Jessie said. "If the Apache return before I do, you'll have the best chance of helping these poor people. And besides, maybe I can hear something about Alton and Juara Madrid. The Mexican Army ought to be familiar with the most dangerous Apaches in this part of Sonora."

"I wouldn't count on that," Ki said skeptically. "And I would not like you to go alone to find that Mexican garrison. Dr. Holt should accompany you."

Jessie's eyebrows raised in question because Ki had never disobeyed her orders.

"If it pleases you," Ki added.

"All right," Jessie said. "We'll leave as soon as the day cools. But I'll need at least some rough directions. This is an easy country to get lost in."

Ki pointed to an old, old man snoozing in the shade of a little tree. "He knows where this military outpost is to be found. Ask him to draw you a sketch in the dirt."

"How about with a pad and pencil?" Holt said.

"If he'll use it," Jessie said, "that would even be better."

Ki led the way over to the old man. "Señor?"

The old man snorted fitfully. Flies buzzed around his sombrero and landed on his bare feet. He did not feel them.

"Señor?" Jessie asked loudly.

Ki nudged the man's bare feet and stirred the old man into wakefulness. Quickly, he explained their need.

"It is many, many miles away," the wrinkled old man began, squinting up through silver brows at them. "And the soldiers, they would not help us. They also fear the Apache. So they stay close to where they live."

"I will buy weapons from them," Jessie said. "And perhaps even hire a few to leave the army and come to fight with us."

The old man shook his head. "This they will not do," he said. "They are very afraid of the Apache."

"Sometimes," Ki said, "money brings courage to men."

"You have much money, señor?" the old man asked.

"No."

The old man shrugged his round shoulders. "You do not have much brains either, or you would not be here when the Apache return to cut off your balls."

Dr. Holt snorted and even Jessie smiled. Ki showed no change in his expression. "You will draw them a picture of how to get there," he said.

The old man shrugged again and held out his hand. Ki thought he wanted money but handed him a little stick instead. "Draw."

The old man drew a river and then mountains. "The river is called Rio de la Concepción," he began. "It feeds the valleys. There are other villages like this."

"And are they also at the mercy of the Apache?" Jessie asked.

"This I do not know."

"How far?" Holt asked. "To this river?"

"Three days walk, two days on horse."

"And then we just follow it through the valleys to . . . to where?"

The old peon pointed toward the southwest. "It is very far. Another two or three days. I don't remember."

Jessie frowned. "So, we're talking four days down, a day or two there, and four back. Nine or ten days altogether. I don't like being away that long."

"It will take at least another week to train these people how to shoot with any accuracy," Ki said. "So we need almost three weeks, and better four, before the Apache return."

Jessie knelt before the old man and said, "How long this time before they come again?"

"I don't know. No one knows except the Apache."

"Big help he is," Holt groused. "Do you think we can even believe that story about the river and the valleys?"

"I believe it," Jessie said. "I've heard of the Rio de la Concepción and the rich valleys and many villages its life-giving water supports. We'll find it. I'm not worried about that half as much as I'm worried about Ki and these people we'll be leaving behind."

"If the Apache come before you return," Ki said, "they will not take us by surprise, but we will not try and fight them. To do so would be to invite a slaughter. We will wait until we have trained these people with the weapons you bring back."

Jessie nodded. She strode off to make preparations for their journey.

"Well," the doctor said, "we came down to find her old family friend, and we wind up chasing ever deeper into Old Mexico after some weapons on the faint hope that they might save these poor villagers. Seems to me that we are going from bad to worse."

Ki understood the man, but he shook his head in disagreement. "Look around you," he invited. "See the misery and the swollen bellies of these people? You are a doctor. A man sworn by oath to help the sick and the dying. Well, these villagers are sick and dying."

"And I've helped them."

"Yes," Ki agreed. "But for what? To be starved and slaughtered for untold more generations? Dr. Holt, what we must do—if we really care for these people and those that will come long after—is to teach them how to protect themselves from the Apache. Only then will we have made any difference."

Holt jammed his hands deeply into his pockets. "I know you're right," he said after long reflection, "but I'm afraid that putting guns into their hands will cause even greater problems. And think of this—if they still lose—the Apache will take such a vengeance that they might even slaughter the women and children. The old men too."

"I do not think so," Ki said.

"Why not?"

"Then who would raise the corn for them?" Ki asked. "Who would weed and irrigate and turn the soil each spring? The Apache? Never."

"Yeah," Holt conceded, "I guess you're right about that. It'd be like the queen bee killing off her workers. Without them, she'd starve."

"Exactly so," Ki said.

Dr. Holt left then to make his own preparations for leaving. Ki watched him and Jessie later that day, when the sun began to slide into the eastern hills. He struggled to hide his worry. Dr. Holt was a brave man and probably an excellent shot with his six-gun, but he was not an outdoorsman who understood the dangers that they might face traveling south.

Jessie, of course, was savvy, courageous, and very resourceful, but she was still a woman and not as physically strong as a man. Besides, Ki worried that there was almost as much danger from the Mexican soldiers as there was from the Apache they might encounter.

"Don't look so worried about us," Jessie said as she saddled her horse and tied her bedroll behind her cantle. "We'll be fine."

"Watch out for ambushers," Ki said. "There are Mexican bandits that would kill you from the cover of rocks for your horse and saddle. And if you see Apache, do not—"

"Ki," Jessie said, leaning down from her saddle, "stop worrying so much. Just be careful."

The samurai was not worried about himself. "If you do not return in two weeks, I will come looking for you."

"Give us a little longer than that," Jessie said. "Sometimes things we cannot foresee happen on the trail. You know that.

Stay with these people for at least three weeks. We'll be back by then, I promise."

Ki nodded. He was samurai, and everything in him demanded that he stay with Jessie and protect her with his life. But at the same time, she had asked him to remain here, to help these people against their enemies. It was a hard thing to be a samurai in America or in Mexico. The Japanese codes often did not apply. Only being honorable and willing to give one's life remained unalterable to a samurai warrior.

"I will not be idle while you are both gone," he said. "I will prepare the boys so that they will not be so afraid. I will train their minds to be brave fighters."

Jessie dipped her chin in understanding. "*Vaya con Dios,*" she whispered softly before she reined her horse south and galloped out of the devastated little Mexican village.

★

Chapter 10

Jessie and Dr. Holt rode south all night through rough, broken country, without finding water or seeing any sign of habitation. It was noon the following day when they finally came upon a little oasis in the searing desert. Their horses were almost staggering from thirst, and both Jessie and the doctor had to restrain them from drinking too much.

Holt removed his hat and sleeved sweat from his brow. "Horses are about played out," he said. "And there isn't a hint of feed in this desert country."

"That's why we've each brought a sack of oats," Jessie said. "Let's see if we can find some shade close by. We'll take a nap and let the horses rest until dark, then fill our water skins and push on."

"I sure hope that old man wasn't lying to us," Holt said. "If we got out there somewhere and there was no river . . . well, it'd be a hard way to die."

"There's a river straight ahead," Jessie said. "It's big and it's deep. It's just a a matter of finding it, and if the old man was right, we should do that sometime early tomorrow morning. Afterward, all we have to do is follow it through the valleys and villages until we come to the Mexican garrison."

Holt returned his hat to his head. "You sure do have a way of making hard things sound easy."

"Over there," Jessie said, pointing to an high cutbank fronting a dry riverbed about two hundred yards south. "We can use that shade to rest and feed the horses."

She rode over to the shade and dismounted, then began to unsaddle the chestnut mare she'd bought in Yuma. The mare was visibly trembling with weariness, and when Jessie lifted her saddle from the animal's back, it groaned with pleasure and shook all over.

Jessie removed her bridle and haltered the animal before pouring about five pounds of oats into a feedbag and tying it to the mare's head. Dr. Holt followed Jessie's example, and when their horses had emptied their feedbags, the animals rolled in the warm sand before they were tied.

"Here," Jessie said, digging into her saddlebags for a paper bag filled with dried prunes and jerky. "You must be hungry."

The doctor wrinkled his nose at the unappealing food. "One will plug you up; the other will do just the opposite."

"Then it's a wash," Jessie said, setting the food down carefully and taking a big chew of the jerky. "Either way, it won't spoil in this desert heat and it'll keep us going until we come to a village and can buy some fresh meat and vegetables, hopefully some hay for the horses."

Jessie arranged her saddle in close to the cutbank and stretched out in the shade. "I'm going to sleep until after dark," she announced. "I'd suggest you do the same."

"You mean we're both just going to sleep right out here in Apache country?"

"We've got to sleep sometime," Jessie said. "And I'm trusting to the fact that if Indians came, our horses would get excited."

"But you don't *know* that!"

Jessie doused a handkerchief with water and pressed it over her stinging eyes. It felt wonderfully refreshing.

"No," she said. "I don't really know if these horses would warn us of danger or not. But since I'm played out, I'm willing to take a chance. And I suggest you do the same. We're not going to be much good tonight if we don't get some sleep."

Holt shook his head. He didn't like the idea of them both sleeping, but even as he was telling himself that it was foolish, he yawned hugely.

"Maybe I'll just rest my eyes too for a few minutes," he allowed.

Jessie closed her eyes, and before she drifted off to sleep, she heard the doctor's deepening snores.

Jessie awoke in darkness to hear the sorrel mare nickering anxiously. The hair on the nape of her neck stood on end. She could not see danger, but she could feel it coming out of the night.

"Doctor," she whispered, crawling over to ease her hand down on his mouth lest he awaken loudly. "Doctor, wake up!"

Holt started badly, and Jessie thought he would have blurted out something in his confusion if she hadn't covered his mouth.

"I think company is coming."

He was instantly alert. "Who?" he whispered.

"Most likely they're Apache coming in for the water."

"They'll see us for sure!"

"Let's try and lead our horses up this dry wash. If we can get just a few hundred yards up, we can hide until they leave."

"But what if they *don't* leave?"

"Then we will," Jessie said. "Anyway, this is not the time or the place to ask questions. Come on, let's saddle our horses, gather up our things, and clear out!"

Holt did not need much urging. In just a few minutes they had their horses saddled and bridled again and their bedrolls and saddlebags lashed down tight.

Their horses were getting more nervous with each passing second, and it was Jessie's greatest fear that the animals would whinny and betray their presence. She still did not know who was coming, but if it were a large body of Apache and if they were mounted, then there was a very real possibility that the horses would become unmanageable.

"Put your hand over the animal's muzzle," she whispered. "Just lightly but if it starts to—"

Too late! Holt's mount whinnied loudly, and suddenly they both heard Apache shouts and the sound of hoofbeats drawing closer.

"Now we're in for it!" Jessie cried, springing into her saddle. "Let's get out of here!"

The doctor from Yuma was in full and complete agreement. By the light of the moon, Jessie saw him vault onto the back of his own horse.

"Which way!"

There really was no choice except to go charging up the dry wash bed with its steep sides. Unfortunately, the wash was narrow and choked with old pieces of wood and tumbleweeds. Jessie spurred hard and prayed harder that her racing mount would not fall or break its leg as it flew over obstacles that suddenly loomed up before them.

She glanced back over her shoulder to see the dark silhouette of her friend, and even though it was too dark to see the expression on his handsome young face, Jessie was sure that he was as frightened as herself.

"Where the hell is this taking us!" he cried.

"I don't know! But anywhere is an improvement."

The dry wash suddenly veered to their left, and Jessie's horse threw itself over a pile of rocks, almost unseating her. Dr. Holt was not so fortunate. His horse did not clear the rocks, and its hind legs landed in their midst. Jessie heard a sickening pop of the animal's leg bones, and then the horse screamed in pain and somersaulted.

Holt was thrown completely over the falling animal. The doctor struck the ground hard and rolled.

Jessie reined her mare to a skidding standstill, then turned it around and went back. She could hear the sounds of the Apache somewhere behind them, and Holt's poor mount was squealing in pain. The doctor, however, was still on the ground.

Jessie threw herself from her saddle, hanging on to her reins so that her own frightened animal did not bolt and race off, leaving them both stranded.

"Don!" she cried, dropping down on one knee beside him. "We've got to get out of here!"

The doctor mumbled something unintelligible as Jessie hauled him to his feet. "Come on!"

Holt nodded, but even in the poor light, Jessie could see that the man's face was bloody and he was dazed.

"Here!" she said, dragging him over to her horse and actually grabbing his left boot and hauling it up to her stirrup. "You've got to try!"

Dimly, Holt seemed to at least be aware of the terrible urgency. He struggled into the saddle, chin resting on his chest and face bloodied. "My medical kit," he whispered. "Don't leave it!"

Jessie drew the six-gun on her hip and shot the suffering horse twice in the skull. Then she jumped forward, untied the medical kit, and somehow managed to swing up behind the doctor. "Let's go!"

She kicked the mare hard and they shot up the wash, the mare laboring to carry them both and still jump the rocks and brush.

Jessie clung to the doctor, as much afraid of him fainting and falling as she was of the poor chestnut mare going down. She knew that they could not run very far before the mare would give out completely.

"We're in a desperate strait!" she called.

He mumbled something she could not hear, but it told Jessie that the doctor was still dazed and would be of little value in a gunfight.

The mare ran until Jessie began to feel her legs buckle. Jessie reached around and drew the mare up, then jumped to the bottom of the wash and pulled the doctor down beside her. She listened intently and heard the Apache closing in.

Jessie yanked her rifle, saddlebags, and a water skin free, then slapped the mare hard across the rump.

"Hiyahh!" she shouted.

The horse, no longer carrying their combined weight, bolted and ran on up the river wash.

"What the hell are we going to do now?" Holt asked, trying to stand up but weaving badly.

Jessie searched both sides of the wash, looking for a place to hide, guessing that she had no more than two or three minutes to get her and the injured doctor to cover before the Apache came racing up after them.

Chapter 11

"Come on!" Jessie cried, shoving the dazed physician up the wash as she desperately searched for a place to hide, even as the sound of the pursuing Apache horses filled her ears.

It seemed as if they had to run a mile before Jessie saw a tangle of twisted wood and brush left by some earlier flash flooding. There wasn't even time to look back to see if they were about to be ridden down by the Apache as Jessie and Holt dove into the debris and burrowed in like desert rats.

"Stay down!" Jessie shouted, fearing that Holt, in his dazed and confused state of mind, might actually try to jump up and run when the Apache came thundering past.

A full minute passed before the Indians on their hard little ponies did come barreling around a bend. Jessie could hear the labored breathing of their horses, who strained through the deep sand. An Indian screamed something unintelligible and the wash was filled with Apache thunder as the horses charged past, some actually flying over the tangle of wood and brush where Jessie and the doctor were hidden.

Jessie waited until there was no doubt that all of the Apache had gone by, and then she crawled out from under the debris. Tearing off a limb, she knelt beside the doctor. "Are you all right?"

He shook his head. There was just enough moonlight so that Jessie could clearly see his bloodied face. He looked pale and sickly. "Don," she whispered, "can you understand what is happening? The Apache will soon catch my mare, then backtrack searching for our tracks at first light. We *have* to put some distance between ourselves and this place."

"All right."

"Here," Jessie said, helping the man to his feet and trying to support him while she scooped up her rifle, water, and saddlebags. "Can you carry the water skin and your medical kit?"

"Yes."

"Okay," Jessie said, trying to calm herself and think clearly because there was absolutely no room to make any mental errors. They were on foot in this harsh Mexican desert with a band of Apache less than a mile away. The Indians had probably already overtaken her sorrel mare. They'd realize their quarry was on foot and could not go far or fast.

"We're going to get out of this wash and without leaving any trace," Jessie said, searching for an escape. "We're going to brush out our footprints as we climb out."

"Okay," he said, trying to sound hopeful.

Jessie knew that things were *not* okay, but there was no sense in worrying about what might happen come first light. So, for the next fifteen minutes, they retreated, brushing away all sign of their tracks until they found an easy exit from the dry wash. The stars overhead were as thick as falling snow when they angled southwest, heading for Rio de la Concepción.

"We'll never make it back to Ki and that Mexican village," Jessie said, trying to hide her deep concern about Dr. Holt's physical and mental condition. "But if we can reach Rio de la Concepción, we have a good chance of floating down to a large Mexican village."

"What then?"

"We attend to your head injury."

"In a poor Mexican village?" The doctor smiled sadly. "I wish it were that simple. The truth is, I've a severe concussion."

"Are you sure?"

"Yes," he answered. "I've all the symptoms. Confused state of mind. Terrible headaches. Dizziness. Cold sweats."

He took a deep breath. Jessie wanted to hurry him. She would have even liked to try to run a little, but she knew that the doctor was having more than a little trouble just staying upright. His balance was faulty, and she had to link her arm through his to keep him moving.

"So what do you prescribe for a concussion?"

"Rest," he said thickly. "Lots and lots of rest."

Jessie could have guessed. "I promise you'll have it," she vowed. "You're going to be all right."

He stopped so suddenly that Jessie was pulled off balance. "What's wrong!"

Holt shook his head. "How far is it to the river?"

"I'm not sure," she admitted. "But it can't be too far. We just have to keep moving. We can't let up now."

The doctor wasn't listening. "Jessie," he said, "I can't allow the Apache to get their hands on you."

"We can talk about that if and when the time comes," she said.

"I know, but if it becomes obvious that they will capture us," he said very deliberately as if he had been thinking about this very hard, "then I must shoot you in the brain so that they cannot . . . cannot make you suffer. And then I will shoot them until I have just one bullet left, which I'll use on myself."

"Don't talk nonsense! The river might be just up ahead. And even if it isn't, it will be impossible for them to locate our tracks until first light. By then, we'll have walked at least ten miles and that's a long ways. We ought to be at the river by then."

He said nothing, but when Jessie glanced sideways at his pale, battered face, she could see that he did not believe they had any chance of surviving. Jessie would not have given them much chance either, were she a betting woman. But as for his declaration that he would kill her and then save his last bullet for himself, well, she had other plans. Jessie would fight to the last bullet and then submit to capture rather than commit suicide, because as long as there was life, there was hope.

They stopped and rested just before daybreak. Jessie brought out the jerked beef from her saddlebags, and they washed it down with water. Dr. Holt's condition was worsening. He had begun to stumble and the last few miles had been a real trial. Jessie knew that if they did not find Rio de la Concepción by nine or ten o'clock this morning, either the Apache would overtake and kill them, or Dr. Holt would collapse. In the latter case, Jessie would have a very difficult decision to make, because there was simply no way that she could escape without leaving poor Dr. Holt behind.

"Do you see the river yet?" he asked, stopping to watch the break of day seep across the barren eastern foothills.

"Not yet," she said. "Dr. Holt, we've *got* to hurry! We've only a few more hours. Every minute is precious. The Apache will have picked up our tracks and will be coming fast."

He cradled his head between his hands. "My skull feels as if it has been opened up like an egg and hot fire poured inside. I'm sick to my stomach and having terrible dizzy spells."

She took his arm. "Just keep trying for another hour or two."

"Listen, Jessie, why don't you go on without me? Try and save yourself. I'll stay here. Fight 'em to the end. Give you more time that way."

"I don't want to hear that kind of talk! We got into this together and we'll get out of it the same way."

"You know what?"

"What?"

"I almost believe you."

"You'd better," she told him. Jessie glanced back over her shoulder. No sign of the Apache yet. Maybe they'd have an even more difficult time finding the tracks than she'd dared to hope. "Come along, Doctor. Time is wasting and the day will soon be very hot."

He didn't want to go, but maybe it seemed easier than objecting. At any rate, Holt leaned on Jessie and they started walking again, the only sound being that of their feet sliding across gravel.

Jessie lost track of time. Like Holt, she had also lost her hat, and now the blistering sun beat upon them without mercy. Within an hour after sunrise, the temperature had soared into the nineties and Jessie was sure that it would soon be over one hundred degrees, long before noon.

Would they even be alive by then? No, she glumly concluded, unless they found Rio de la Concepción very soon.

After an hour of walking, Jessie made a decision. "We need to seek out a high vantage point," she said. "If the river is in sight, then we might make it yet."

"And if we don't see the river?"

"Then we'll make a stand," Jessie decided.

"I'm seeing double," he told her. "I couldn't hit anything with a gun or a rifle. I wouldn't know which image to aim at."

"Shoot between them," Jessie said. "Or shut one eye and aim. I don't know. You're the doctor. You figure that one out."

He dredged up a weary smile. "I've never met a woman as beautiful and at the same time as strong as you are, Jessie.

And no matter what happens to us this morning . . .”

“Shut up,” Jessie said wearily. “There is a good-sized hill up just ahead and you’re going to need all your breath to climb it.”

“Whatever you say,” he replied, his face wintery and white.

It took them nearly a quarter hour to reach the hilltop, and Holt crawled the last few hundred yards.

Jessie still could not see any sign of pursuit, but she knew that, like the sands in an hourglass, time was quickly running out for them.

“Come on!” she urged, proud of the doctor for trying so hard. “Just a little farther.”

“That’s what you’ve been telling me for the last hour!”

“Yes, but this time, I really mean it!”

When they topped the rocky hill, the climb proved worth all the pain. “Look!” Jessie cried. “There it is! Rio de la Concepción!”

Holt stared, his eyes wide open. “Two rivers!”

“Close one eye,” Jessie advised with a smile, “and then pray that we can get down there before the Indians overtake us. Let’s go!”

Now hope gave them newfound strength. Holt surged to his feet, and Jessie wrapped her arm around his waist as they staggered down the hill toward the river, which she judged to be still a good mile away.

Holt was inspired by the sight of the great desert river and its promise of escape from death. Face crusted with dark blood, eyes rolling crazily around as he tried to hold focus, the man churned through the deep, hot sands as they lurched downhill and across the final stretch of desert.

“Are you sure it’s not just a mirage,” he gasped at one point. “If it is . . .”

“It’s not!” Jessie cried. “We’re almost there and it’s no mirage.”

Rio de la Concepción flowed wide and deep. It would never rival the Colorado, Mississippi, or the Columbia rivers, but it was bigger than anyone could have expected in this harsh Sonoran Desert.

"We're going to make it!" Jessie cried. "We'll build a little raft for our guns and ammunition to keep dry, then we'll—"

A rifle shot sounded across the desert, and Jessie whirled around to see Apache galloping hard after them. There were six, perhaps seven, of them, and they were closing the distance in a big, big hurry. Jessie shoved Holt into a staggering run.

"Come on, we can still make it!"

The Apache unleashed a bloodcurdling scream, but Jessie kept the doctor moving forward. Her heart was slamming in her chest, and she did not think that they would make it to the river. And even if they did, there was no guarantee that they wouldn't be shot by the Apache from the bank.

Jessie cast a desperate glance over her shoulder. The Apache were now in rifle range, and the river was yet a good two hundred yards away. They weren't going to make it before the Apache rode them down.

"Go on!" Jessie cried, breaking loose from the doctor and dropping flat on the hot desert floor. "Run!"

"But . . ."

"Go, damn you!" she cried, taking aim at the lead rider and then squeezing off a shot.

The Apache took a bullet high in the shoulder. He screamed and tumbled from his horse. Jessie fired again and another rider was unhorsed. The charge broke. An Indian leaped from his running horse to fire his rifle. Jessie took a deep, calming breath. The smell of gunsmoke was thick in her nostrils, and the barrel of her Winchester was hot to the touch. She fired, deliberately aiming low.

91

The Apache grabbed his leg, howling and hopping around. The others threw themselves from their ponies and took cover in the sagebrush.

Jessie jumped back to her feet. She left the water skin but took her saddlebags and the doctor's medical kit. Without a backward glance, she sprinted on. In less than a minute, she overtook the poor doctor, and they staggered on the rest of the way to the river.

They plunged into the cold current, hearing the angry howls of the Apache. Bullets began to puncture the surface all around them, and Jessie, keeping her rifle overhead, squatted down in the river until only her head and shoulders were visible.

"Swim!" she shouted to the doctor. "Swim for the middle and let the current carry you downriver!"

Holt began to thrash into deeper water as Jessie levered another round into the Winchester. The remaining Apache had remounted and were now galloping along the riverbank, shouting and firing from their lathered ponies. They shot rapidly, but Jessie thought there was little danger of being hit by one of their errant bullets.

Jessie planted her swollen feet in the river-bottom mud. She took aim and unseated another Indian. The Apache realized that they could not hope to hit her while on horseback and jumped to the ground. Jessie winged one more, then reluctantly dropped the Winchester rifle into the powerful current and began to swim downriver for her life.

Bullets ricocheted off the surface of the water all around her, but the distance between Jessie and the Indians rapidly widened as the river carried her away. Jessie knew that she and Dr. Holt had at least a chance of escape. There were only a few Apache left that were not wounded, and she still had a Colt in the holster strapped to her hip. It might not fire wet, but if she had been an Apache, she would not have bet her life on it.

"How are you doing!" Jessie called, overtaking the doctor, who had wisely adopted the practice of floating most of the time just underwater, showing his head only when he needed to take a fresh lungful of air.

"This beats the hell out of crawling in that desert!" he shouted.

Jessie agreed. The water was cold, and it breathed new life and hope into her. She managed to kick off her boots, which weighted her down.

"Much better without the boots," she called to Holt.

He nodded. A bullet struck the surface just inches from their faces. Holt dove underwater and Jessie thought it wise to do the same. Underwater, the world was silent and protective. Jessie wished she could remain underwater for hours. It seemed incomprehensible that only minutes ago she had been staggering across a burning desert.

Holt and Jessie surfaced at the same time, and to their relief, they saw that the Apache were still far up the river, their pursuit blocked by fallen trees and heavy undergrowth. Jessie sighed with relief, and when she looked at the doctor, she saw that the black blood had been washed from his face and he was actually smiling.

"We got a chance now!" he called. "I think, unless this river goes underground, we can just float all the way down to the Sea of Cortez."

The Sea of Cortez, as the Mexicans called it, was more popularly knowing in the United States as the Gulf of Mexico. "Is that where this river ends?"

"I sure hope so! Those bloody bastards will play hell shooting us out of that much water!"

Jessie laughed. In spite, she waved farewell to the Apache, who howled all the louder with frustration. She looked up at the bright, hot sun. God, she thought, it was wonderful to be alive!

Chapter 12

The Apache vanished at midmorning, and Jessie was sure they did so because she had not only killed but also taken deliberate care to wound several of their number. Those wounded would have to be taken care of, perhaps even transported to some distant Apache village where they would be administered to by a medicine man.

Dr. Holt's condition had improved for about two hours in the cold river water but then deteriorated. The coldness had seeped into bones, and as soon as the Apache vanished, Jessie struggled to bring Dr. Holt onto shore.

"Here," she said, opening her saddlebags and pouring out the river water. "Eat some jerky and dried prunes. They'll give us both some badly needed strength."

"The jerky," he said, eyeing it critically, "is starting to get soggy and come apart. And I hate prunes."

"I know. Eat them anyway. You need food to keep your strength."

He was too weak to do much more than nod his head, then gaze off into the direction in which they'd last seen the Apache. "Will they come back and hunt for us?"

"I don't know," Jessie said. "If they rule the villages we hope to find all along this river, then I'd suspect they know that's where we can be found. I'm worried that we might bring hardship on innocent villagers."

"What choice do we have but to seek their help?"

"None," Jessie said, deeply concerned over the way that the handsome young doctor had begun to shiver. She was afraid he was going into shock.

"I'm sorry that you lost your medical kit," she said.

"I didn't lose what was in it," he said, patting his pants pockets. "At least not the most important things such as my scalpel, forceps, needles, and suture. But I lost all the quinine and the river took care of my headache powders. Fortunately, the laudanum was in a watertight tin. I'd use some now except that I'm afraid of the complications that might take place given my concussion."

"I had to give up my rifle," Jessie said with a sad shake of her head. "But I've still got my pistol and about twenty rounds in my cartridge belt. We'll make it."

He nodded, but his teeth had begun to chatter and he was shaking so violently that Jessie helped him up to the dry, hot sand to rest in the shade of a cottonwood tree. She looked downriver, wishing she had some idea of how far they were from the nearest Mexican farming village. It might only be around the bend; then again, it might be fifty miles.

"The prunes," he said, chewing slowly, "are almost as tough as the jerky—but I'm not complaining."

"Sure you are," Jessie said, shielding her eyes and looking up toward the sun. "After we rest and warm up a little, we're going to have to get back into that river and keep going."

He stared at the river. "It saved us once, maybe now it will deliver us unto a Mexican Garden of Eden."

"Don't count on it," Jessie said, her thoughts on Ki and the little Mexican village they'd left to the north.

There was a secret sleeve sewn into the lining of her saddlebags, and she opened it, then removed a thin bundle

95

of hundred-dollar bills along with several twenty-dollar gold pieces. The gold, of course, was fine, and it might be the only currency that the villagers would accept.

"If the soldiers or the villagers won't take soggy American cash," Holt said, "we can always use it to light our camp fires."

"I can't say about the villagers, but the officers will know how to spend it," Jessie said with assurance. "And if we don't come upon a village by this evening, I'll have to risk a gunshot and hunt us some supper."

"What about using some of my suture and a hooked needle as a line and fishhook?"

Jessie smiled. "Your teeth may rattle and your poor, battered face is the color of a headstone, but your brain is still in good working order, Doctor."

"Thanks," he said, "but it doesn't feel as if it's working at all."

Jessie patted him on the arm. "I'm going to make us a little raft or something that we can hang onto and where we can put our guns and ammunition. If we need them suddenly, it won't do to have them wet."

"What if the gunpowder is wet?"

"It probably is," Jessie said, "and if I had to guess, I'd say it couldn't be fired. But the powder ought to dry inside the cartridges if they're in the hot sunlight."

"That's taking a lot for granted, isn't it?"

"Yes," Jessie said. "I've dropped a loaded gun in a river, picked it up, and then fired. But our weapons have been underwater and are probably out of commission."

"Great. Just great." Holt closed his eyes. "My head is pounding like a hammer against an anvil."

"Just rest easy while I make a raft," Jessie said. "It shouldn't take more than a half hour and then we'll be ready to get back into the water. Must be well over a hundred degrees."

He looked at her. "Your face is burning."

"So is yours," Jessie said. "We'll have to find some way to shield ourselves or we'll be in bad shape tomorrow."

He nodded, and Jessie went off to find something to make their raft.

It took her at least an hour to find enough branches and tule reeds to weave together and then cover with bark. Her raft wasn't big enough to support their weight, but it was large enough to keep her saddlebags and their weapons dry.

Holt slept all the while, and when the raft was ready and Jessie was bathed with sweat, she woke the man up and said, "We've got to go on now."

He nodded, cradled his head in his hands, and groaned. "I sure wish I could just sleep."

"You will," she vowed. "Just as soon as we find a village and someone that can help take care of you. Then, you can sleep all you want and you'll feel much better in a few days."

"It might take a little longer than that," he said. "At least, that's what they told us in medical school."

Jessie supposed the doctor was right. But she'd once been tossed from a bronc and landed on her head. She'd had a severe enough concussion that she'd bled through the ears and also had double vision for the better part of a week. And remembering how slow her own recovery had been, Jessie realized that she would have to leave Dr. Holt to the care of some Mexican villagers and then go on alone to find the military garrison. Holt would object, of course, but she really had no choice. Ki was expecting her back, and the village people he was trying to protect were counting on her for guns and ammunition. They might be attacked by the marauding Apache any day, and therefore, she couldn't have the luxury of staying with Dr. Holt until he was completely well again.

Jessie dragged her crude little raft over to edge of the water. She unbuckled her gunbelt and then the doctor's and placed them in the center of the raft. "We're going to have to be real careful not to tip this thing over and lose our pistols," she warned. "If that happens, we're in bad shape."

Holt nodded to indicate that he understood. "Are you sure that we can't wait until tonight?"

"I'm sure," Jessie said.

"All right then, let's go."

The doctor was so weak that Jessie had to help him into the river, and the moment he was submerged to his neck, his teeth began to chatter violently. Jessie gritted her own teeth. The water was refreshing for the first ten or twenty minutes, but then it started to become numbing.

"We'll go as far as you can, Don. But if you start to feeling too weak to hang onto the raft, let me know and we'll go back to shore. I've gotten you too far now to see you drown."

"I couldn't agree more," he said, grinding his teeth together.

Jessie removed her blouse. She dipped it in the water, then wrapped it turbanlike around her head and face except for a slit for her eyes.

The doctor clucked his tongue as he studied her lovely chest. "I'm seeing four of the biggest, lushest breasts I've ever seen in my life. This double vision does have a few advantages."

Jessie managed a grin, then sank down into the water until only her head was above the surface.

"Why don't you do the same with your shirt and then let's go."

"Will you help me?"

She helped him, and she was encouraged when his mouth playfully found one of her nipples. "You're not as sick as you look, Doctor."

98

"If you wanted to take off everything," he said, "I might even surprise myself with a medical miracle."

"No, thanks." She pulled his shirt tight over his sunburned face. "Let's go for a swim."

They floated all the rest of that day, constantly anticipating that around each bend in the river they'd come upon a Mexican village and green fields of corn. But if they were disappointed not to find help, at least the Apache didn't show up either.

That evening, Jessie carefully removed their weapons and ammunition from the raft. The bullets and their six-guns were still very hot to the touch from the sun.

"I need to find out if our powder is dry again," she said. "And we need some fresh meat if we're to keep our strength."

"Are you sure we can risk gunfire out here?"

"No," she admitted, "but I need to find out right away if we're armed or not."

"I suppose."

Jessie wished like anything for her boots. Barefooted, she would not be able to walk more than a couple of dozen feet into the desert before the soles of her feet would be cut, pricked, and bruised by thorns and rocks.

"Why don't you cut your pants legs off and wrap them around your feet?" the doctor said. "Better yet, just take your pants off and cut them up."

"You'd like that, wouldn't you?" she said with a smile.

"You bet I would."

"I'm beginning to think this is all an act that you're putting on," Jessie said. "But your idea is good."

She sat down and pulled off her pants, then cut the lower half of the legs off. She wrapped them around her feet and tied them with strips from her belt. When she stood up, she knew she looked ridiculous without a shirt and only the cutoff pants.

"Well," she announced as she reloaded her six-gun, "this ought to be very interesting."

"What are you hoping to bag? Pheasant? Venison? Buffalo?"

"Ha! If I'm real lucky, I might come across a rattlesnake. They're good roasted."

He swallowed noisily. "What about sage hen or at least jackrabbit?"

"Not very likely. I'd say there was a much better chance of rattlesnake or even gila monsters."

"You mean those big, fat, ugly and *poisonous* lizards!"

"Supposed to taste as delicious as chicken," Jessie lied. He said nothing more, and she stepped into the sagebrush with the sun dipping low on the western horizon.

Jessie could not go far in the clumsy footwear, and she didn't have to. She had not walked a hundred feet into the sagebrush when she heard the dry, scaly shiver of a rattlesnake. It was a big one from the sound of it, and Jessie's heart beat a little faster as she tiptoed forward, hearing the rattle grow louder and louder. But she knew that rattlesnakes were not very aggressive and most of them would try and get away unless they were cornered.

Parting the brush, she saw the biggest rattlesnake she'd ever seen in her life, and it was like none she had ever seen before. Instead of being brownish gray like the diamondbacks she was familiar with, this one was short, thick as a big man's forearm, and bright green. And it wasn't coiled either. In fact, to her horror, it started coming for her.

Jessie raised her pistol, took aim, and pulled the trigger. The click of the hammer falling on a dud cartridge was as loud in her ears as the gong of a cathedral bell. The snake was amazingly quick. She had never seen anything so aggressive!

Jessie aimed and pulled the trigger once more, but the gun in her fist did not fire. Turning in fright, she took off running. She tripped and fell, climbed to her feet, and ran on down to the riverbank, where a startled doctor was waiting.

"What's the matter!"

"A snake is after me!" She raised her hand and pointed. The green snake was still coming. It was not nearly as fast as a person on foot, but it seemed to have plenty of determination.

"Holy cow!" Holt shouted, jumping to his feet like a man raised from the dead by lightning. "Holy cow, what is it!"

"I don't know! I've never seen a snake act like that before."

"Let's get out of here!"

"Good idea," Jessie said, tossing everything on their raft and shoving it into the current.

She and Dr. Holt were out in the water fast. The sun was just going down and the sky was ablaze with salmon, red, and purple color. But neither Jessie nor the physician was in an admiring mood.

Squinting into the growing darkness, Jessie said, "Can you see it? Did it stop at the water?"

"I sure the hell hope so," Holt replied. "I never saw such a snake in my life."

"Me neither," Jessie said, still clutching her worthless six-gun and squinting back toward the receding riverbank where they'd hoped to make camp. "And I hope I never do again."

They floated several miles until they came upon a low sandbar. It was only about eighty feet long and less than ten feet wide.

"No green rattlesnakes here," Jessie said, pushing their little raft up onto the sand. "Let's camp and get some sleep. We can eat the rest of the jerky and prunes and try to catch some catfish for breakfast."

Holt nodded. He was so tired that his hands shook as he took food from Jessie. The jerky was starting to disintegrate from being wet so long. But the prunes were in excellent shape, and they had six of them.

"It's been a hell of a long day," Holt sighed.

"Yes," Jessie said, "but at least we're still alive to see the end of it."

"Yeah. I need to keep reminding myself. But what if we don't find any villages tomorrow?"

"Then we have no choice but to keep floating."

"Who knows how far it might be?"

Jessie could see that the man's spirits were at rock bottom. Small wonder. He was in considerable pain, seeing double, and looking feverish.

"We'll make it," she said quietly. "I know we will. How's the pain in your head?"

"It's doing just fine. Hasn't missed a beat."

Jessie detected the bitterness in Dr. Holt's voice. He was shivering again, and she wished she could have gone over to the riverbank and floated some dry wood across to their island to make a fire. But that would have created a big and quite unnecessary risk. Besides, while blindly searching for wood in the dark, she might well stumble upon another one of those mean, green Mexican rattlesnakes.

And from what she'd seen, she'd rather come across an Apache warrior any old day.

★

Chapter 13

Jessie spent the first quarter hour of daylight rigging up a needle and suture. They had saved a few pieces of soggy jerky, and when she baited the hook, Jessie said a little prayer that the fish would consider the jerky more appealing than her young companion had.

"I've never been much of a fisherman," she said, stringing out the suture to its full length.

Holt frowned. "It would be a lot better if we had at least two or three more feet of line. A fish can see you from this short distance. Better lie down on the sand and remain very still."

Jessie did as suggested. The fishhook and bait were only about a body length from her hand. She could see the silver surgical needle glimmering in the water and the vile-looking piece of black jerky. There wasn't a fish in sight; nor had she seen one the entire day before while they'd been in the river.

"I'll give it a half hour," she said. "After that, I'm going to tie this damn suture to your big toe and *you* can pull the fish in."

Holt grinned but said nothing. They both watched the shining fishhook and the piece of jerky twirl slowly in the shallow current. They also kept a close watch on the shore just in case the Apache returned.

It was only about eight o'clock and the heat was starting to build. After a half hour of patiently waiting, there still wasn't any sign of a fish—or the Apache.

"What do you think?" Jessie asked.

Holt looked at her through suffering, bloodshot eyes. Last night she had inspected the wound on his scalp, and it was deep. Jessie feared that it might become infected, but perhaps the river had kept it cleansed.

"I think you need more patience," the doctor told her.

"Are you still seeing double?"

He nodded and watched as Jessie looked anxiously over her back and studied the riverbanks for Apache.

"Here," he said, taking the line from her hand. "I've always been uncommonly lucky with a fishing pole."

"We don't have a pole and no worms, either."

"Hungry fish aren't that picky," he said, taking the line.

Jessie eased back from the water to stand up, because the doctor had explained that fish could see shadows passing overhead. She walked to the other side of the sandbar, then waded out into the river and sat down, cooling herself off. This was a hard country—nothing green except the trees and a little grass hugging the riverbank, beyond that, just ruined bluffs and barren, sun-blasted mountains. It looked to her to be so hard that even coyotes would starve.

Jessie dipped her head in the river and scrubbed her sun-burned face. She unbuttoned her blouse, then wrapped it around her head and face again, but that left her bare shoulders and chest vulnerable to sunburn. What she wouldn't give for her Stetson or even an old sombrero.

Turning to look down Rio de la Concepción, she willed herself to imagine a big, prosperous village just beyond the next bend. There, they would find someone to take care of Dr. Holt until he recovered from his concussion. Perhaps they'd also find Mr. Lamont and Juara Madrid, who would tell them how they'd escaped from the Apache raiders and taken sanctuary. And finally, they'd be taken to the Mexican garrison, where Jessie would charm a handsome young Mexican officer into delivering weapons to the beleaguered little village just in time to save it from destruction.

Jessie dunked her head in the water again. Sure, she thought, and fairy tales always come true.

"Hey!" the doctor shouted. "I got one!"

Jessie twisted around to see the doctor hauling in a huge catfish. The fish was thrashing wildly on the sandbar, and then it broke the suture and went cartwheeling across the sand.

"Get him!" the doctor shouted, trying to scramble after the big fish.

Jessie surged to her feet and joined the doctor as they both scrambled after the flopping fish. Twice, they had it pinned under them, but the slippery cat squirted out of their grasp and managed to dance to the water's edge.

"He's getting away!" Jessie cried as she and Holt dove headfirst into the shallow water and they pinned the squirming fish between them, then managed to scoop it back up onto the sand.

Jessie pounced on the fish, and it squirmed into a trap between her large breasts. It felt awful!

"Have you got him!"

"Yes, but get him out!"

The doctor reached under her and fondled her breasts for a moment before he managed to hook his thumb and forefinger into the catfish's gills. Then he expertly snapped the fish's head back and Jessie heard its spine pop. The fish stopped thrashing and quivered in death.

"We got him!" Holt said with a broad smile as he raised the big cat. "But boy did he ever give us a fight!"

Jessie nodded. She could feel the slime of the fish on her chest, and she turned to go back into the water and wash, but the doctor grabbed her by the wrist and fell on her.

"You were wonderful," he said. "It would have got away for sure if you hadn't jumped right in the middle of it."

"Thanks."

He bent his head to her breasts and sniffed. "Smells a little fishy."

"I know. And if you'll get off me, I'll wash."

His smile faded. "I want you right now."

"You're crazy," she protested. "We're both half-starved, dirty, and smelly. What—"

He wasn't listening. Dr. Holt's lips found her fish-smelling breast, and he began to suck softly, using his tongue on her nipples.

"This is insane," she whispered. "You shouldn't be doing this. You're not a well man."

"I'll feel a lot better in a few minutes," he said, unbuttoning her pants and then his own before he pushed her legs apart and mounted her.

Jessie wiggled her bottom in the hot, wet sand. He felt good inside of her and she tried to ignore the fish smell. When he began to move over her, the slime made their bodies extremely slick, and they got to laughing about how he kept sliding off.

"Here," she whispered, wrapping her long legs around his plunging hips. "That ought to keep you in place."

He groaned deep in his throat as his thick rod stirred her passion higher and higher. This time, it was Jessie whose body lost control first. She cried out in ecstasy and felt a hot, liquid fire erupt deep in her loins. A moment later, she felt his warm seed fill her womanhood and she milked him energetically.

"Ahhh!" he moaned, going limp, then rolling off onto his back, closing his eyes to the rising desert sun. "If we have to die, let it be right now and I'll have no complaints."

"Well, I will," Jessie said, rolling over on her side and studying his battered face. "Besides, we're not going to die.

106

We're going to find a village and get out of this alive."

He did not open his eyes, but he did smile. "Do you think so, Jessie? Do you really think so or are you just saying that to prop up our sagging spirits?"

"We'll make it," Jessie said, pushing to her feet. "But we can't lie here and burn up in this sun. Let's take the fish and swim across to the opposite riverbank. We'll roast the fish and—" Jessie's words died on her lips. "We can't make a fire!"

"Has that just now occurred to you?"

Jessie nodded. "I've been so preoccupied thinking about how we are going to find a Mexican village and get out of this mess that I didn't give a thought to cooking a fish."

"Well," he said, "I've heard that Indians consume flesh raw and I think that I am hungry enough to do the same."

Jessie's stomach flopped, but she had to admit that he was right. Their food was gone except for a few last prunes she found, and they needed nourishment. This big catfish would sustain them another full day.

"I'll wash and cut the meat into strips. If we had time, we could leave it in the sun and it would cure. But since we're in a hurry, we're going to have to eat it now."

Ten minutes later, the fish was cut into strips, and they lifted it to their mouths. To Jessie's surprise and relief, the raw flesh was quite delicious; not something she would eat regularly, but the meat was chill and firm, really quite good.

"We should probably save some of this," she said, "but I'm counting on reaching a village before tonight."

"And if we don't," he said, "we'll find another sandbar, make love two or three times while we fish."

Jessie chuckled. "I'm beginning to think that your concussion has caused you to live in a fantasy world."

But he shook his head and his smile died. "There's nothing 'fantasy' about all of this, Jessie. It's hard, brutal, and my head still feels like it's splitting down the center. But with you at my side, I know that we're going to overcome anything we face. That includes Apache and green rattlesnakes."

Jessie was touched by his sincerity. "You're not so bad to float the river with either. But we'd better be on our way. I'm worried about Ki and that village. I told him we'd return in a few weeks. Time is passing and, so far, we've managed to get ourselves deeper into trouble than when we left the samurai."

"You told me that he'd be fine."

Jessie turned to let her green eyes drift off to the north. "He won't allow the Apache to kill what few men remain or to rape any more women," she said. "And yet, the samurai knows that he can't really defend the village without arms. If the Apache return before we bring rifles, I don't know what he will do to protect those people."

Holt nodded. "Come on," he said after a few moments of grim silence. "Let's find some help for all of us."

★

Chapter 14

It was a long, hot day, and again, the doctor grew steadily weaker as the cold river sucked away his strength and will. Twice, Jessie had to pull him up on the bank and insist that they lie in the hot sun for fifteen or twenty minutes while she rubbed his bluish limbs in order to stimulate circulation.

"You can rub a little lower," he said through chattering teeth.

"That's *not* where I want to increase your circulation," she scolded, knowing he was trying to raise both their spirits. Privately, she was not sure that he could survive another day of floating in the cold, swift river. More and more frequently, she was watching to make sure that he didn't just sink under the water and drown.

"Quit worrying so much about me," he said, reading the fear in her eyes. "I'm going to be just fine. I'll find me a fat old señora that can cook good frijoles and toast tortillas, and I'll be back on my feet in no time."

"Sure you will," Jessie said, rubbing his arms hard and seeing the way his cheeks and eyes were sinking into his face. It was a good thing, she thought, that he could not see himself, because, being a physician, he'd know that his health was rapidly failing. The only good news was that his deeply lacerated scalp had still not shown any sign of infection.

Jessie rubbed his body until he seemed to revive a little. "There's a log just upriver," she said. "It's the first I've seen that doesn't look so waterlogged that it would sink like a rock. I'm going to walk up the bank and try and push it into the current. If I can do that, you can climb up onto it and not have to use so much energy trying to stay afloat."

"You really *are* worried about me, aren't you?"

"You just need some rest," she told him. "Besides, you can't be that bad off given your randy behavior."

He chuckled weakly. "Just wait until I get a few platefuls of beans into my belly."

"I can hardly wait. Be right back."

Jessie climbed to her feet and hurried back upriver. The log was a quarter of a mile off, and when she came to it, she was dismayed to see that it was half-buried in the muddy riverbank. She found a stick and began to scrape away the mud that held the log, and it took her nearly a half hour to dig the thing out. Then, she had to use every bit of her remaining strength to roll the log deeper into the current so that it would float. It was a heavy thing—eight or nine feet long and as big around as her waist. Jessie rolled the log over and over in the current to clear off the dirt and mud, then walked the log down along the riverbank through the shallows until she returned to Holt, who was watching with approval.

"Our ship is ready," she told the man, pushing the log into the bank and gathering her saddlebags and her six-gun with the questionable cartridges that had not fired earlier.

She tied her little reed raft to the log, and between the two, they had quite a sizable little flotilla. "Up on the log," she ordered.

Holt was so weak that it was all he could do just to flop across the log and lie on his belly, cheek pressed to the rough bark. Jessie shoved the log and raft back into the river until the current lifted her off her feet; then she also jumped onto the log and let it move deeper into the river's channel until they were moving rapidly with the current.

The sun's glare on the water burned her poor eyes until they wept and stung. She removed her blouse and again wrapped it around her head and neck. The cloth shielded her eyes somewhat, but she had to squint all the time from the surface glare, and she could feel her bare shoulders burn. It occurred to Jessie that if they did not come upon a village by tomorrow, not only were they going to be blind and fried, but they'd be in even more serious trouble. Especially the doctor, who was steadily weakening even now that he no longer had to do a thing except lie on the log and rest.

Dusk found them rounding a great horseshoe bend in the river, and suddenly, with the sunset bathing a huge agricultural valley, they floated down toward a big Mexican settlement. They saw children playing on the riverbank, and Jessie quickly unwound her turban and pulled on her blouse. The doctor, who had fallen into a fitful slumber, did not awaken until the children's shouts became quite loud.

"What!" he cried, startled into wakefulness. "Apache . . ."

"No," she said, throwing an arm around his shoulders, "it's all right! We found a big village. You're going to be all right!"

From the little adobe shacks came an outpouring of villagers, and Jessie noticed at once that there were many men, telling her that this village was strong enough or on good enough terms with the Apache to be protected.

The women and children stared and pointed at Jessie, and then several of the men waded out and helped her and the doctor to shore. It was immediately apparent that the doctor was too weak to stand. Orders were given to take him at once to a resting place under a shade tree. Women hurried back to their little adobes to grab tortillas and corn.

111

A strong drink was offered and Jessie did not decline. It burned a fire down her throat, and after so many hours in the cold river, that felt very good.

In her best Spanish, Jessie explained how she and the doctor had come to float down the big river to this place. She also told the wide-eyed villagers about their fight with the Apache and how they had barely escaped with their lives.

This piece of news caused immediate alarm among the people, who began to talk so rapidly that Jessie had great difficulty even understanding them. But clearly, they were suddenly very worried that the Apache would come to this village, seeking them, and that they would be held accountable for helping Jessie and the white man.

"Listen," Jessie said, trying to assuage their mounting fears, "the battle that I describe took place two days ago and many miles from here. Right now, we need your help. As you can see, this man with me is very, very sick. He is an American doctor. If you help him, I am sure that he will help you when he is feeling better. He can save many lives. You *must* help us."

The older men of the village looked very doubtful. They stepped off to one side and went into a little huddle. They were not in agreement, and Jessie could hear them arguing back and forth on whether or not to risk their own people in order to help her and Dr. Holt.

Jessie looked to a young woman about her own age. "I understand that there is a Mexican Army garrison somewhere to the south of this place. How far, señorita?"

She was a lovely young woman with raven hair and large, expressive eyes. Eyes that betrayed curiosity rather than fear.

"It is one day by boat," she told Jessie. "Longer by foot or on a burro."

"Straight down the river?"

"*Sí.*"

Jessie heaved a deep sigh of relief. "And how many soldiers?"

The girl shrugged her shoulders. "I do not know. Many, I think."

"Do they have horses?"

"Some."

Jessie nodded and turned back to the doctor. Tomorrow morning, she would hurry south to find this Mexican garrison and attempt to buy rifles and horses enough to carry them north to the village where Ki was waiting for her return.

"Jessie?"

"What?"

Holt was trying to stop shivering, and Jessie took his arm and began to rub it vigorously. The beautiful Mexican took the doctor's other hand and began to do the same.

Holt looked up at her. His Spanish was not as good as Jessie's, but it was good enough to be understood. "What your name, señorita?"

"Margarite."

"Now," he said, "I have two angels to admire. How blessed I am!"

The young Mexican woman blushed deeply, and she could not meet his eyes, but she did rub his arm even harder. Jessie felt a twinge of . . . of what? Jealousy? Envy that she could not remain here to rest and take care of Dr. Holt's needs during his recovery? Perhaps she felt both emotions. One thing was abundantly clear and that was that Dr. Holt was going to be well taken care of no matter what the old men decided.

The elders had reached their decision by nightfall, and after a simple but very substantial meal of corn tortillas and beans, they came to stand before Jessie, faces grave.

"Señorita," one of them said, "we are a peaceful village. The Apache, they come often and they take what they want

113

but they do not hurt us. We live with them in peace."

"You live under their rule and pay them homage. How much corn or animals do you have to give them each year?"

The old men stiffened. They did not like to be reminded of this and were offended.

"We give them what they want to eat, but not our women or children," one said defensively. "It is only food that they take. Maybe too a horse or a dog. Nothing more."

"Why give them anything they have not earned?" Jessie demanded. "I intend to buy rifles so that another village very far to the north can fight to keep what they grow."

The old men exchanged worried glances. "You do not understand," one said after a minute or two had passed. "You know nothing about this village."

Jessie sighed. "You're right. It's not my place to tell you how to live. If you choose to be subjected to a ransom for your safety, then that is what you should do. But I thought the Mexican government had vowed to protect you against the Apache."

One of the old men, a short, heavyset fellow dressed in a red serape and wearing sandals, cleared his throat. "The soldiers, señorita, are more to be feared than the Apache. We have no use for them. They come and get drunk and use our women."

The old man spat in the dust between them. "The soldiers are swine. You should not go to them for help."

"Then who?" Jessie asked.

The elder shrugged his thick round shoulders. "You should go away and not come back. If the Apache come here and find you, we will be punished. Maybe a few of us will even die."

Jessie expelled a deep breath. "I understand," she told them, choosing her words carefully. "And I *will* go away. But you can see that the doctor is very, very sick. He must stay and

114

you must care for him until he is strong again. In return for this, I will pay you well."

Then, Jessie reached into her saddlebags and extracted the twenty-dollar gold pieces. At the sight of them, the old leaders of the village drew in a sharp breath. Jessie saw the longing in their eyes. Maybe they had never—in their entire lives—seen so much wealth. And the thought that it might soon belong to the village was almost beyond their comprehension.

"I will give you one of these now and another when I return," she told the elders. "A third one I will give to those who help me deliver the rifles to the village in the north. A village where all the men have been killed by the Apache and which now lives so poorly that the people are close to starving because the Apache steal almost everything they grow."

Jessie studied their faces. "Maybe," she added, "they once had a strong village like this and were willing and able to fight the Apache. But then, they grew afraid and their young men were all killed. Now, they are only women, children, and elders like yourselves. It is a very sad thing. You must think about this while I am away."

The old men nodded. Jessie extended a gold piece and it was taken with bows of gratitude.

"We will help your friend grow stronger until you return. But if the Apache come while you are away . . ."

"Then you must hide him from them," Jessie said quickly. "Hide him or they will kill him and then maybe kill you."

The old men nodded in worried agreement. Jessie told them her plan to leave early in the morning. They were not pleased and looked extremely worried.

"Do not let them make you afraid," the young man named Margarite said that evening when they prepared to go to sleep. "The old men have seen many bad things. Long ago, we were like the village you spoke of."

"So what changed things?"

115

"We fought the Apache. It was before I was born. Before even my mother was born. We fought them with arrows, stones, knives, and spears. And we killed many."

The young woman swallowed. "But now, the Apache have rifles and guns. They could kill all of us if they wanted and our weapons would be useless. They know this and so do we."

"And yet, they let you live."

"We feed them very well," the woman said, "and sometimes, they catch one of us and they have their pleasure."

Margarite's eyes brimmed with tears. "And then there is nothing that anyone can say or do. So we just pray and hope it does not happen again too soon."

Jessie instinctively reached out and touched the girl's arm. "I am sorry."

Margarite brushed her hand away and jumped to her feet. "I will go see if your friend needs food or drink," she announced. "He is very thin."

"Yes," Jessie said. "I hope that you can fatten him up while I am away."

The girl turned in the firelight. "You might never return," she said flatly. "The soldiers are even worse than you have been told. They are animals. Even the officers. Maybe you should go back to the United States before it is too late."

"It is already too late," she said. In a few words, she explained about her father's old friend and the young half-breed named Juara Madrid. "Have you seen such men?"

"No," she told her. "Not for many weeks."

Jessie started. "Then you actually have seen them!"

Margarite's eyes softened. "Come," she said, extending her hand to Jessie.

Jessie took the woman's hand and they walked out to the edge of the village. The stars were a glittering blanket of diamonds, and somewhere out in the vast, cruel Sonoran Desert,

116

a coyote howled and was joined in a mournful chorus.

"This," the girl said, "is where my mother and father are buried."

The cemetery was very old. Some of the graves were covered with rocks and without headstones. Others had simple wooden crosses over them. A few were fresh, and at one of them, the girl stopped.

"The old man you described," she said. "He is buried here."

Jessie's heart fell. "Are you sure?" she asked in a hushed whisper.

The girl nodded her head. "He was brought to this village by the half-breed that you describe. He was wounded and dying. The Apache left him here and told us to try and save his life because he was very rich and maybe they could get him to send to the United States for money. But he died."

Jessie knelt before the grave. She silently vowed that, if she survived Mexico, she would get in contact with the family of Alton Lamont III and tell them this story. She said a little prayer for the old man who had earned the respect of so many. He had been generous and kind. He deserved much better than to lie in this unnamed Mexican village in a pauper's grave so far from those he loved.

When Jessie came to her feet, she felt empty and sad. "What about the young half-breed?"

"He has become one of them," Margarite said. "He is Apache now. A man I think will someday be a leader."

Jessie took this news hard. After all, Mr. Lamont had died because he had been trying to help Juara Madrid. They had been planning to own a horse ranch together. Jessie had sensed a deep friendship, almost a father and son relationship, between the unlikely pair.

"Why do you think that he will become a leader?"

There was a long pause before Margarite said, "Because he is strong and wise."

Jessie studied the girl closely, but her face was a mask. Margarite hurried away, leaving Jessie alone beside the grave with more questions than answers.

★

Chapter 15

Jessie awoke to the smell of frying tortillas, beans, summer squash, and corn. She rubbed the sleep from her eyes and stood up, feeling stiff and battered. Even though she'd slept nine hours or more, she still felt very tired and realized that the physical and mental strains she'd undergone these past few days had taken their toll. What she needed was to stay here and rest for several days before continuing on downriver. But what she had to do was to leave at once.

"Señorita?" a soft voice called into the little shack where she had slept that night.

Jessie rolled out off the straw pallet and combed her hair with her fingers. She knew that she must look a fright and that she badly needed a new blouse and pants. However, it was very unlikely that she'd find either in this poor Mexican village.

She snatched up her saddlebags and walked outside, shielding her eyes from the rising sun. An old woman, face brown and wrinkled and hands like burned lumps of dough, smiled toothlessly at her and motioned for Jessie to be seated.

A child, shy and pretty, dashed forward with a clay jar filled with cool goat's milk, which tasted wonderful. Jessie was served on a wooden plate big mounds of food that she consumed with a very unladylike appetite.

As she ate, the elders came to watch, and when she raised her hand to indicate to the old woman that she could not consume another morsel of her wonderful cooking, the same old Mexican, with the sad, rheumy eyes, bowed and removed his sombrero, then gave it to her with a smile.

"I cannot take this!"

"Please," he begged. "Your face is so beautiful. It is unwise to burn it like meat in the sun, no?"

"Yes," Jessie had to agree. She placed the sombrero on her head. It was, of course, several sizes too large and it rested on her ears, but she was grateful.

"*Gracias*," she told the man and the old woman who had cooked for her.

Jessie picked up her saddlebags. She would make a very quick stop to say good-bye to Dr. Holt and then she would have to depart, no matter how reluctantly.

But the elders of the village pressed around her and their spokesman gave a sharp whistle. At once, everyone turned to see a boy lead a fine mustang forward. It was a smallish bay horse, but its ears were pricked forward and it walked with a lively step. Two stockings and a blaze face made it a pretty little horse, and it wore an old Indian saddle and blanket along with a fine silver bit.

"It is for you," the old man explained. "Maybe this horse will bring you good fortune. Maybe you will need him to get away from the soldiers. I don't know. Only God knows."

The villagers nodded in agreement and most made the sign of the cross.

"I'm very grateful," Jessie said, meaning it with all her heart. "The idea of getting back into the river and floating down to the garrison was something I was dreading."

The elders nodded with understanding, and their leader said, "There is one officer. His name is Señor Jose Alvarado. He is

120

an officer and a man of some dignity. You must look to him and him alone for help."

"Is he the commander? The *comandante* of the garrison?"

"No, señorita," the Mexican said with a sad shake of his head. "But he is the only man that has respect. You seek him out."

"I will. If I leave now, will I be there by nightfall?"

"On this horse, *sí*!"

Jessie extended her hand and shook with each of the men. Then, she patted the old señora on the shoulder and went to say good-bye to the doctor.

He was awake and waiting for her. At her entrance, Margarite nodded and quickly left the room so that they could be alone. The doctor looked very weak and unwell this morning, but Jessie said, "You look much stronger."

"No I don't," he replied. "But by tomorrow, I should start to show improvement."

"The beautiful girl that is tending to your needs will make sure that you have anything that you want."

"I hope so," he said, managing a wink.

Jessie scoffed. "You're a rascal and a rogue, Dr. Holt."

"You ought to know." He took her hand. "You could have left me behind out in that desert a hundred times. I thank you for my life."

Jessie blushed. "You'd have done the same if the situation was reversed and I had the concussion."

"I'd like to think so."

Quickly, Jessie told him about the little mustang pony and the advice that she should seek out Señor Jose Alvarado. "They seem to believe he is a very good and decent young man. If so, I can use his assistance."

"Don't trust any of them," the doctor warned. "You'll be a foreigner and very much at their mercy."

"I know, but—"

"And once they realize that you are carrying around a bundle of one-hundred-dollar bills American money—soggy or not—the temptation to take it from you by force will be almost irresistible."

"I know that too."

"Then please," he begged, "can't there be some other way to—"

"No," she said, "there's no other way. Ki and those villagers must have rifles."

"Then let's go back to the United States and buy them!"

"It would be too late by then." Jessie forced a smile. "I'm going to be fine, Doctor. Just relax, eat plenty, and rest. You'll need to be well again when I return with the Mexican muskets."

He tried to smile but failed miserably. "All right," he said. "It will be a struggle just lying here all day and night with that homely girl in my attendance. But I'll try to cheerfully endure my hardships."

Jessie laughed and bent to kiss the doctor. This time, he did not even fondle her breasts, so she knew that he really was quite unwell.

Everyone was waiting in a big semicircle around the mustang when Jessie reappeared. The boy held the reins of the spirited horse while Jessie mounted and her stirrups were lengthened to accommodate her long, shapely legs. She tied her saddlebags behind her cantle, and one of the women handed her up a leather bag of hot tortillas and several ears of corn on the cob. Another man tied a skin bag of water to the opposite side of the saddle.

"Adios!" she called, and they all repeated the cry.

Then, Jessie kicked the flanks of the mustang and it bolted forward into a fast gallop. She flew past the little adobe where Margarite was waving good-bye and aimed the mustang south on a rutted road that paralleled Rio de la Concepción.

The wiry little mustang was strong and it liked to run, even in the punishing heat. Jessie had to hold the animal in now and then for fear it might run itself to death. Four or five times that day, she reined the horse over to the river and let it drink greedily.

By late afternoon, the wind was blowing hard and there were dark clouds on the horizon. Jessie was riding directly into the storm, and she knew about the torrential downpours that could take place in the desert and was careful not to ride in the dry washes that led down into Rio de la Concepción.

It was almost dark when she saw the Mexican fort nestled on a low bluff overlooking the river. By then, she was being pelted by the first drops of rain, and had it not been for the leather tie under her chin, the sombrero would have sailed away.

A jagged bolt of lightning split the dark, ominous sky. It stabbed into a pile of rocks and exploded with a blinding light. The mustang whirled away in fright, almost unseating her.

Jessie got the animal under control, speaking to it in a soft, reassuring voice that had the desired effect.

"Easy, boy. Easy now."

It was raining hard as the sun vanished, and when Jessie approached the pathetic little fort with its six-foot-high crooked pole walls, she saw no sign of any sentries. The gate was open for anyone to enter, and she did.

The walls encompassed an area perhaps fifty yards wide and twice that long. To her right were low adobe barracks, and straight ahead was what she imagined to be the officers' quarters. There was also a guardhouse, corrals, and a barn, all crudely constructed and looking as if they would blow down in a high wind.

The rain was falling so hard by the time she dismounted that it washed away even the mustang's spirit and Jessie led the animal over to the barn.

Inside the barn, three soldiers were playing cards on the bottom of a barrel by the light of a flickering candle. When Jessie entered, they did not even bother to look up from their game, but when she tied the horse and stepped away from it to remove her sombrero, one glanced in her direction and his mouth fell open with surprise.

"Good Lord!" he exclaimed. "A gringo woman!"

The man who had been dealing out the hand froze and stared. He was fat, dark, and sinister looking. His uniform was even dirtier and more tattered than those of his companions and he wore no boots, not even a pair of sandals.

"Eii-chi-wah-wah!" he exclaimed, rising so quickly that he knocked the barrel and the cards over. He didn't notice. His eyes were as big as his loose, lascivious smile as he started for Jessie.

She took a backstep and then her hand flashed to the Colt on her hip. The gun came up, and its barrel lined up directly on the fat soldier's wide chest.

"I will kill you if you come another step closer," she warned.

The man froze in mid-stride. Jessie's voice was hard enough to make him think twice about what he instinctively had in mind to do to her in a bed of straw.

"Ah, señorita," he wheedled, "surely one as beautiful as yourself has been sent from heaven to fulfill Miguel Ortega's nightly dream."

"Surely not," Jessie said, keeping her gun trained on the man. "I want you to go and tell a Señor Jose Alvarado that there is a woman here who must speak with him at once."

"But—"

Jessie cocked back the hammer, and the barrel of her gun dropped an inch. Ortega's eyes bulged with alarm when he realized that her pistol was now aimed at a spot directly between his fat legs.

He paled. He threw his hands up in the air and cried out with fear before wheeling around and lumbering out the door.

"You two can sit down and pick up those cards. Start playing again."

The soldiers didn't look very interested in playing cards, but when Jessie turned her gun on them, they went for the cards as if they were nuggets of gold.

Jessie waited impatiently for nearly a quarter of an hour. Finally, she heard the rapid thump of boots outside, and the door was pushed open to reveal a scowling officer.

"Who are you and what do you want!" he demanded.

Jessie was taken aback by the sternness in the man's voice. "Are you Lieutenant Jose Alvarado?"

"I am Captain Escobar!" the man shouted. "Lieutenant Alvarado has been confined to his quarters! I am in charge here and I demand to know the meaning of this!"

Jessie took a deep breath. "Can we talk in private?"

Escobar had a long mustache and the nervous habit of rolling its tip. He sighed and relaxed. "Very well. Put away that gun and follow me to my quarters."

Jessie holstered her gun and started after the man, but when she reached the door, a soldier grabbed her, threw her to the mud, and landed on her hard.

"What are you doing!" she cried as her gun was taken away and her hands were jerked up behind her back. "Stop it!"

Escobar looked down at her in the pouring rain. "I don't know what you want or where you came from but we will find out!"

He looked to one of the other grinning soldiers. "Bring her saddlebags to my office and do not open them!"

The soldier nodded and Jessie was hauled to her feet. "This is outrageous!" she cried. "I'm not here to pose any threat to the Mexican Army. I come to ask your cooperation."

"And you draw your weapon on my soldiers?"

"I had to!"

Captain Escobar wiped a smear of mud from her face. "You are a very beautiful woman. Let us also hope that you are a very cooperative and intelligent one."

Then, he turned on his heel and marched back across the compound, leaving Jessie to be dragged along behind.

She wanted to scream she was so angry! What kind of a *comandante* was this! And why was Lieutenant Alvarado confined to his quarters? Had that anything to do with her arrival?

All these thoughts passed through Jessie's mind in a swirl of turmoil. She was angry and . . . yes, very afraid. She was at the mercy of these people, and she had little faith that they would treat her with any more respect than they would a whore.

★

Chapter 16

Jessie was shoved headlong into a filthy office where the captain obviously slept. A very large woman was snoring loudly on his bunk, face to the wall. Her clothes were strewn about the floor, an empty tequila bottle resting on her underwear.

The captain marched up to his desk and whirled around to face Jessie. "Release her!" he ordered his soldiers.

Jessie was freed. She was so angry that she was shaking. "What is the meaning of this! I came to speak to you on a civilized level and I'm treated like a criminal!"

"You pulled a gun on Sergeant Ortega!" the captain shouted.

"I *had* to! He was coming at me."

"That is not the story he tells."

Jessie forced herself to speak calmly. "Could we speak in private?"

The captain nodded to his soldiers, who started to turn away but halted when Jessie said, "I want my saddlebags—now!"

"Put them on my desk," Captain Escobar barked.

The saddlebags were placed on the captain's littered desk. Jessie forced herself to remain quiet as she watched the man open the saddlebags and empty them. Captain Escobar quickly pawed through her belongings and inspected a few items, only to discard them with obvious disappointment. Her secret money compartment was not discovered, and the captain tossed the saddlebags at Jessie's feet.

"Who are you?" he demanded.

She told him her name, expecting he might have heard of the Starbuck empire, but he displayed no interest or recognition. That was just as well. Jessie had no intention of enlightening this man about her personal fortune. He was, she judged, a poorly educated man who would probably attempt to ransom her for his own personal gain.

"Why are you here, Miss Starbuck?"

Jessie chose her words carefully. Now that she had seen how ruthless this commanding officer acted, she wasn't about to let him know that she was carrying hundred-dollar bills.

"I have come to ask you to lead your men north where a village is constantly under siege by Apache. It is a small village of no more than a hundred."

"Describe it."

Jessie quickly described the village. "It has no name."

"Yes it does, Señorita Starbuck." The captain twirled the tips of his mustache. "The village is called La Rosa, though there is nothing of beauty there to give it the name of a rose."

"Its beauty is in the people who are being plundered and robbed by the Apache."

"The Apache raid many villages like La Rosa. The people know that they must either pay a tribute, or else learn to protect themselves. Mexico City cannot do everything."

"Everything?" Jessie mocked. "You are doing *nothing*!"

"You speak out of ignorance, señorita! You know nothing of Mexico. You do not belong here!"

"Perhaps not," she conceded, "but the people of La Rosa are living in terror and privation. Their women are being taken away and any of the men who dare to oppose them are shot."

"Life is hard in Mexico," he said coldly. "Go back to New York City."

Jessie clenched her hands at her side. Yelling and losing her temper with this pompous fool was not going to get her anywhere. "You could be there in three or four days to help them."

"Ha!" Escobar laughed. "The Apache would see us coming long before we arrived. If they did not set a trap and slaughter my soldiers, they would simply wait until we left La Rosa and then attack it again—only harder, to punish the people for seeking the army's help."

"Are you telling me that the Mexican government will do nothing to protect its own people?"

The captain shrugged his round shoulders. "It would be a waste of time and government money. If those people are afraid of the Apache, then they should go away. If they lived close to us, we could help them. But as it is . . . impossible. I am responsible for my soldiers."

"So what *do* you do?" she demanded. "Besides live in this pigsty?"

Escobar's swarthy face darkened with barely suppressed anger. "You have a sharp tongue. Maybe I need to teach you how to serve an officer of the Mexican army. Maybe I will throw Donita out of my bed and you will take her place!"

"I would rather die first," she hissed. "Touch me and I'll scratch your eyes out."

The captain paled. He took a threatening step forward, but Jessie did not retreat or show any sign of fear—only anger. This caused the captain to have second thoughts.

"You are a handsome woman in a bad place," he said, "and you appear to be too stupid to realize that, without my cooperation, you will never leave this place alive."

Jessie knew that they were fast approaching a stalemate. She was afraid that he would fly into a rage if she insulted him again and that she would be overpowered by the soldiers and then raped and confined in their guardhouse for months or even years.

"Listen," she said, "perhaps we have gotten off to an unnecessarily bad start. But if you would just consider going to the aid of the people in La Rosa, then—"

"In this weather?" The captain shook his head. "Too wet. My men would catch pneumonia and sicken."

"Then perhaps when the weather clears?"

He shook his head so violently that his double chin wagged and his rapierlike mustache tips twitched. "It will be too hot then."

Jessie's contempt for this man knew no boundaries. "So you intend to do nothing."

"Correct," the captain said. "You see, we have more important villages to protect."

Jessie would have bet her entire Circle Star Ranch that this man protected nothing save his own hide.

"If I could find cash, would you sell me rifles, ammunition, and horses?"

He blinked. "That would take a lot of money, señorita."

"How much? I would want at least fifty rifles and five thousand rounds of ammunition."

The captain's eyes narrowed. "I don't have repeating rifles even for my own soldiers. We use muskets. But they are good and accurate."

Jessie had expected as much. It would still be some years before the cartridges replaced black powder and balls among the poorer Mexican soldiers and citizenry. Muskets were cheap and far more readily obtainable. Furthermore, since they were becoming obsolete in the United States, thousands of old cap-and-ball weapons were being transported south and sold very cheaply to the people in Mexico. Moreover, cartridges were much more expensive to fire than black powder and lead.

In many ways then, and despite the fact that the raiding Apache were sometimes armed with stolen repeating Winchesters and Colt revolvers, there were distinct advantages to arming the people of La Rosa with inexpensive and dependable old muskets rather than more modern repeating rifles.

"All right, muskets then."

"How much money are we discussing?"

"A thousand dollars." Jessie had figured ten dollars each for the muskets, ten more for the ammunition.

Captain Escobar's eyebrows shot up. He grinned. "You are talking a lot of money!"

"More than you make in three or four years, I'll bet," Jessie said.

He nodded. "Where would you get this money?"

Jessie had anticipated this question but still did not have a good answer. If she told the man that she had a thousand dollars hidden in her saddlebags, he would simply rob her. If she didn't convince him she had the ability to raise one thousand dollars, he might well dismiss this entire conversation.

"I will have it when you arrive in La Rosa."

"Ha!" he laughed mockingly. "You must think I am a fool to believe such a story."

"It is true!"

"No," he said. "Without money first, I would do nothing to help."

"Can I think about this overnight?"

"What good would that do?" he asked. "Would the money suddenly appear like an angel?" The captain shook his head. "Señorita, I am beginning to think that you have been in the sun too long and have suffered too much. You should stay here with me and rest. We can enjoy each other's company."

Jessie needed time. If she refused his advances, she would not doubt be locked in the guardhouse. After that, there was no telling what might happen to her. She realized that she either

131

had to escape this place, or else find and speak to Lieutenant Alvarado. Perhaps he would help her.

"What about Donita?" Jessie said, looking over at the snoring woman.

In reply, the captain marched over to the woman, grabbed her by the arm, and yanked her off the bunk. Her head banged hard against the floor and she woke up cursing the captain. The woman was very fat, probably weighing over two hundred pounds, and she attacked Captain Escobar. The pair stood toe to toe, swinging and cursing at each other. The woman connected solidly and rocked the captain back on his heels, but he recovered in time to call his guards before she could completely overpower him.

"Lock this *puta* up!" Escobar raged. "Lock her up and feed her swill!"

"Touch me and I'll kill you!" Donita screeched.

The guards hesitated, sending Escobar into a fury. He wiped blood from his smashed lips and shouted, "Get her now!"

More guards were called in, and Jessie watched as they all charged the fat woman and drove her to the floor. She bit one man's arm to the bone and raked another's face so terribly that he ran out the door screaming with blood all over his face.

But the the sheer weight of their numbers overpowered Donita, and she was finally subdued, bound, and then dragged outside.

The captain slammed the door shut. He looked badly shaken and his lips were pulp. "That bitch will pay for this!"

"Let me help you," Jessie said, going over to a basin and pitcher of water. "Sit down."

When the captain slumped in a chair, Jessie picked up the pitcher of water and poured it over the man's head.

"Hey!" he cried.

Jessie grabbed the heavy clay pitcher and smashed it down on the man's skull as hard as she could. The pitcher shattered, and Captain Escobar collapsed in a pool of water.

Jessie took a deep breath, then found a piece of rope. She bound and gagged the captain, then closed her eyes for a moment and tried to gather her wits. She had to find Lieutenant Alvarado and see if he could help her. If he could not, she had to escape and be long gone this stormy night before the captain was found and his soldiers sent after her.

"What have I gotten myself into now?" Jessie said, staring down at the corrupt officer lying at her feet. She snatched up her saddlebags and her six-gun, which had been placed by the soldiers on Escobar's desk.

There was no turning back now, she thought, one way or another, I have to be gone before morning or I am a dead woman.

★

Chapter 17

Jessie had no idea where to find Lieutenant Alvarado or, even if she did, if he would be of any help to her and the people of La Rosa. But if he were confined to his quarters, then he must be in some kind of trouble and perhaps he could be persuaded to assist her in exchange for a new life north of the border.

She removed the captain's coat and pulled it on. She found his hat, then shoved her hair up under it. Stepping to the only window in the quarters, Jessie was relieved to find it opened easily. She squeezed through the window with her gun in her hand, and through the heavy rain, she studied the compound, searching for the lieutenant's quarters.

She picked out a small adobe next door and saw a light shining through its window. Moving through the rain, she went to the window and peered inside to see a handsome young man pacing anxiously back and forth. Was this Alvarado and would he help her? Jessie wasn't sure. For a moment, she had a strong urge simply to make her way to the stable, get the drop on anyone who might still be there, and make her escape into the night.

But something about the young officer inside changed her mind and made her slip around the adobe to the front. There, she took a deep breath, said a small prayer, and pushed open the door.

Jose Alvarado whirled and started to say something, but then he realized he was staring at a woman dressed in his *comandante*'s clothing.

"Who are you!"

Jessie closed the door behind her. "I'm a woman in trouble. I have been told you are sympathetic to the Mexican villagers. That you are a good and a reasonable man, unlike Captain Escobar. Is this so?"

He shook his head as if to ensure that he was not dreaming. "I . . . I don't know about that," he said. "But the captain and I do hold different opinions. In fact, I am under arrest. Were I an enlisted man, I would be huddling in our muddy guardhouse under a leaking roof. But . . . but what has all this to do with your presence here?"

Jessie told him in as few words as possible. She ended by saying, "The people of La Rosa need help. I know that you cannot force the soldiers to go there against their will."

"And they would not if asked," he said. "They fear the Apache as much as the villagers."

"Then help me take some muskets to the villagers."

"Steal them from the armory?" The lieutenant shook his head. "I am not a thief!"

"Then I will pay for them," Jessie said. "Captain Escobar allowed he would sell them to me, but he'd have kept the money for himself."

"You could pay for them?"

Jessie nodded. She reached into her saddlebags and opened the secret little compartment where she kept her money. "Here. A thousand American dollars. I want you to help me deliver at least fifty muskets and plenty of ammunition to La Rosa."

"Even if I could do this, I would be court-martialed and executed by firing squad."

135

"Then desert this corrupt army and come to the United States," she said. "I own a ranch in Texas. I promise you work. Whatever you can do. You can take it or I will help you find other work in a town. I have many contacts. You will live a far better life than this and you will help the people of La Rosa so that they never again live in fear."

"What you ask is impossible!"

"Is it?" Jessie removed the captain's hat. "Nothing is impossible if you try hard enough. Is there anyone else that you could trust to help us?"

The lieutenant shook his head.

"Are you sure?"

"I am sure." Alvarado frowned. "You see, this post is manned by ex-convicts from the prison in Mexico City. They can either stay in prison, or come here for five years. Many, knowing the hell of this country, elect to remain in prison."

"If it's so bad, why were you sent here? Are you being punished for some reason?"

"I killed two of my fellow officers," Alvarado said. "It's a long and ugly story. You don't want to hear about it."

"You're right," Jessie said. "There's no time for that now and it's none of my business. All I want to know is if you will help me get some muskets and ammunition and deliver them to La Rosa."

"In return for . . ."

Jessie hid her disappointment. She had been naive to think that this man would help out of the goodness of his heart. "A job or enough money to buy yourself a small business."

"I would take the money. How much?"

"Five hundred dollars."

His dark eyes glittered. He was tall and lean with a hawkish nose and a prominent jawline. He looked far more like a Spaniard or Italian than a Mexican, and there was an air of danger about him. Jessie could easily see why a self-serving

136

little official like Captain Escobar would find this junior officer very threatening. And the fact that he had killed two of his fellow officers would be very unsettling to the captain.

"I would like half of the money now, half when I help deliver the muskets and ammunition to La Rosa."

Jessie counted off two hundred dollars. "Three more upon deliver. Mr. Alvarado, allow me to remind you that time is wasting. We're going to need a good, long head start."

He took the money, and Jessie kept her hand on the butt of her Colt because she did not yet trust him.

"You stay here," he said. "I will take care of everything and then—"

"No. I want to come along. Just in case."

"In case what?" Alvarado asked. "On a night like this, there are no guards. They are all sleeping in their beds. And tomorrow, if the rain holds, they will refuse to come after us."

"But the captain will—"

"Will do nothing," Alvarado said, his voice dripping with contempt. "He is afraid of the soldiers, who would slit his throat if he tried to force them to go more than ten miles in the rain or near the Apache."

"Are you saying that no one will try to stop us?"

Alvarado found a heavy coat and his hat. He scooped up an old black-powder Navy Colt and a worn holster and strapped the belt around his lean waist. He pulled his coat over the pistol to keep it dry.

"I did not say that there is no danger," he told her. "If we are caught, we will both be executed. But I do not intend to be caught. And we will leave money with the captain, which will make him decide that silence is his best reward."

"All right."

Jessie followed Alvarado out into the rain. The man walked swiftly through the mud, and when they were almost to the stable's door, Jessie caught up with him. "There were three men playing cards in here an hour ago. One of them was Sergeant Ortega. If he is still here, he will try and stop us."

"Ortega." The lieutenant spat the word out like a watermelon seed. "Few things would give me more pleasure than to kill him."

Jessie grabbed Alvarado by the sleeve. "Listen," she said urgently. "I don't know or even want to know what you've done here to get into trouble or the reasons why you hate Ortega. All I want is to get fifty muskets to La Rosa. Is that understood?"

He looked down at her, and then he grabbed and pulled her roughly to his chest. His mouth found hers and he kissed her hard, bruising her lips.

"Damn you!" Jessie swore, slapping his wet face. Thunder and lightning crashed across the dark heavens, and the wind grew stronger. The rain began to come down in horizontal sheets, and it was cold and cutting.

Alvarado didn't seem to notice. He touched his smarting face, grinned, then turned and drew his pistol before stepping into the barn. To Jessie's dismay, the three soldiers had resumed their game of cards. When they saw Alvarado and her, they went for their guns.

Alvarado shot the sergeant in the center of his broad chest. The man spilled over backward and thrashed around in a stall. A bolt of lightning crashed somewhere nearby, and Jessie prayed that Alvarado's shot would be mistaken for part of this terrible storm.

"Pull those guns and you will join your sergeant," Alvarado said.

The two other soldiers threw up their hands. They both looked ready to faint with fear.

"Turn around," Alvarado ordered.

"Don't kill them," Jessie said, totally at a loss to predict what this man would do next.

138

Alvarado threw her a smile; then he stepped forward and struck both soldiers very hard with his pistol.

"We need to saddle four horses," Alvarado said, jumping forward. "Then we'll lead them over to the armory. We should be gone within the hour."

Jessie nodded and went to help. Her mustang gave her trouble. Perhaps it could smell death, or maybe it simply did not want to be taken back out into the driving rain. Whatever the reason, it took Jessie as long to saddle the little horse as it did Alvarado to saddle three others.

"Stay behind me," Alvarado ordered, handing her the reins to one of the horses and then leading two out ahead.

The storm was so ferocious that Jessie had to lean into the wind and drag the balky horses forward. Half-blinded by the sheets of freezing rain, she plowed ahead through the thick, sticky mud.

"Here," he called into the storm when they came abreast of what Jessie assumed was the armory. "Hold the horses!"

She saw him pull a key from his coat pocket, and it took several moments for him to work the lock open. Then, he vanished inside, only to return a few moments later with his arms laden with muskets. He leaned them up against the armory wall, then rushed back inside for more. He brought out a small barrel of black powder and several heavy bags of lead musket balls.

Lastly, he found heavy canvas bags inside and tied them to the saddles of their spare horses. In this way, they were able to carry the muskets, powder, and ammunition. He divided everything in half and loaded both horses before he covered the weapons and ammunition with canvas and lashed everything down.

Jessie had her hands full just keeping the horses under control. The wind howled and the rain was driving the poor horses to distraction. It seemed to her that it took hours before they were ready to ride, but it actually took less than an hour.

"Let's go!" he shouted.

Jessie needed no further urging. The little mustang tried to drop its head between its legs and buck her off into the mud, then run away, but Jessie whipped the animal hard and sawed on the reins so that the best it could do was to crowhop around in circles. By the time she got it under control, Jose Alvarado was out the fortress gate, heading north.

"Come on!" she snapped at the ill-tempered little mustang. "It's a long, long ride to La Rosa and I've got no patience to fool with you in this kind of weather."

The mustang laid back its ears and charged through the gate, its little hooves hurling globs of mud, several of which struck the ex-lieutenant and his three horses. Jessie heard Alvarado yell after her, but she could not understand his words as she fought to pull the mustang to a standstill.

The horse had other ideas. It took the bit in its teeth and ran. Jessie let it run, and it was dawn before the lieutenant was able to overtake her. With the new day, the storm died and the huge, dark clouds sailed on down toward the Gulf of California.

"That is a crazy horse," Jose Alvarado said. "It is the kind that will get a person killed."

"I guess I should have taken another," Jessie conceded. "But at least he is strong and has a big heart."

Alvarado chuckled. In the light of day and now some twenty or thirty miles north of his Mexican prison, he seemed almost euphoric.

"Life will be better now," he said. "Tell me about this ranch of yours in Texas."

Jessie spent several hours telling him about her herds of cattle and how the ranch had been founded by her father. She talked about her foreman, Ed Wright, and also about Dr. Holt, whom she hoped would be well enough to travel north when they reached the village where he was recovering.

"This Dr. Holt, is he your lover?" Alvarado asked.

Jessie blinked. "I don't really think that's any of your business!"

"Ah, then he *is* your lover. Too bad."

"Why?"

"Because, I would be better," Alvarado said. "And it is a long way to La Rosa, is it not?"

"It is, and if you touch me, I will kill you. Is that clearly understood?"

Alvarado laughed. "I have never taken advantage of a woman who did not want to be taken advantage of. That is not my style."

Jessie found that she believed this man. He was bold, handsome, and virile. And unless she was mistaken, despite his violent background and killings, she was sure that the old Mexican villager had been correct when he'd said that Jose Alvarado was a good-hearted man.

"You're wondering about me, aren't you?" he said, glancing sideways at her. "You're wondering if I will try and kill you for your money. In fact, I could take everything including these muskets. I could sell it all and buy myself a little ranchita somewhere here in Mexico. Change my name and be a wealthy man all the rest of my days."

"I suppose you could," Jessie said, "but I don't believe you will do that."

"Why not? I have already confessed to you that I am a murderer."

"Yes, you confessed. But there was no time for me to ask why."

"Are you asking now?"

She nodded and watched as the sun burned away the raindrops from the tall, stately cactus.

"All three of us were young and headstrong, lions in the heart of Mexico City. We all were from good families and were expecting excellent posts because we had graduated near

141

the head of our class from the military college of Mexico City. And then one night in a cantina, my friends saw and wanted a beautiful young dancer. After her performance, we went back to her dressing room. I thought they would pay her compliments, but they tried to rape her. She resisted and they began to beat her senseless. I tried to stop them. There was a fight. I was knifed and rather than allow myself to be butchered, I drew a two-shot derringer and killed them both. I have always considered the affair a matter of honor."

"And what became of the dancer?"

He shook his head, smile fading. "She never regained consciousness. I would have been executed had there not been other witnesses. Even so, I created a problem for the army. They felt I was a disgrace and so I was banished to this garrison under Captain Escobar, a pig if ever there was one."

Alvarado shook his head. "Privately, I was told that the two officers were two of many of the dancer's lovers and that I should never have interfered on her behalf."

Alvarado was silent for a few minutes before he added, "Sometimes, I think they were right. I lost everything. My father, who was a career army officer and who died at the Battle of San Jacinto, was disgraced. He never spoke to me again and, in fact, was the one to suggest that I be banished to this hellish outpost."

"What about your mother? Was she also shamed, or was she proud?"

Alvarado smiled. "She . . . she died two years before. But I believe that she would have been proud of what I did. I believe that with all my heart."

Jessie involuntarily reached out and touched the lieutenant's cheek. "I believe she would have been proud too. As a woman, she would have been very proud of you."

"*Gracias*," Alvarado said before turning his face away and staring out into the desert wilderness.

★

Chapter 18

It was just after dark when they reached the big village where Jessie had left Dr. Holt. As she and Jose Alvarado rode down the street, the Mexicans came out to stare at her with a great deal of curiosity. Several recognized the former lieutenant and called his name in greeting. It was clear to Jessie that he was a popular man among these people, and that was reassuring.

They dismounted, and men held their horses while Jessie led the way into the adobe to see Dr. Holt. He was sitting up, looking anxious.

"Jessie!" he said. "Thank heavens you made it. Everyone said that we'd never see you again."

At that moment, Jose Alvarado stepped into the adobe. He was wearing his officer's uniform, though his hat was missing and one of the villagers had already given him a serape to keep him from the cold.

Jessie made the introductions and added, "Without Señor Alvarado's help, I would have left empty-handed. He's agreed to help us."

The doctor extended his hand and the two men shook. Alvarado said, "I do not expect pursuit, Señor Holt. Captain Escobar is not . . . how do you say it, filled with gallantry."

"Good!"

"How are you feeling?" Jessie asked.

The doctor looked at Margarite, who hovered nearby. "I'm feeling better. But I still get dizzy when I stand up, and I still see double. I think it might take a few weeks."

Jessie frowned. "You know we have to leave because of the threat to La Rosa."

"La Rosa?"

"That's the name of the village where we left Ki," Jessie explained. "The lieutenant and I brought about fifty Mexican muskets and plenty of black powder and lead balls."

Holt frowned. "It's a shame that you couldn't have gotten more modern firearms."

"I disagree," the lieutenant said, quickly explaining how the cap-and-ball muskets were so much cheaper to use.

"I don't mean to interrupt," Jessie said, "but I'm worried sick about Ki and that northern village. I'd like to leave here the first thing tomorrow morning. All of this will be wasted effort if we don't deliver these arms before the Apache attack."

Holt nodded. "Any word of Juara Madrid?"

Jessie started to shake her head, but Alvarado said, "Juara Madrid? How do you know him?"

Jessie told the man about Alton Lamont and the young half-breed that he had befriended. She ended up saying, "Ki and I met Juara at a stagecoach station called Gila Crossing. I had the feeling that Juara was rather special."

"Oh, he is," Alvarado said. "In fact, I have heard that he is already an Apache leader."

A shadow of disappointment crossed Jessie's face. "I would have thought that he might be a moderating force in the name of peace."

"Apparently, he is," Alvarado said. "Word reached us that Madrid was trying to talk some of the other Apache leaders like Geronimo into seeking a truce with the United States Army."

144

This piece of news was heartening to Jessie. She might never again see Juara Madrid, but she felt as if this news confirmed Alton Lamont's trust and judgment in the young half-breed. And perhaps he would not forget her offer of a job training horses once this conflict between the red man and the white had finally been settled.

"Doctor, I don't want to leave you," Jessie said, "but we have to go. Ki and the people of La Rosa might be under attack this very moment."

"If they are, there is nothing that you can do to help now."

Jessie knew that the doctor was right, but that did not mean that she intended to waste any time going north to the samurai's aid.

"Will you be all right?" she asked.

The doctor nodded. "I want to repay these people for the kindness they've shown me. I'd like to stay awhile even after I'm fit enough to travel and see if I can't take care of some very obvious and debilitating medical problems. There are people who need serious medical attention."

"I'm proud of you for saying that," Jessie said, suspecting that the beautiful Mexican woman who was the doctor's constant attendant might also have a little bit to do with his decision to linger in this poor village.

Margarite leaned close to the doctor and whispered something. Holt smiled.

"What?" Jessie asked.

"She says that I am beginning to look tired and lose color. She is worried that I may become unwell if I don't get a full night's sleep."

"I see," Jessie said, her suspicions confirmed. "Well then, the lieutenant and I had better leave you to your rest, Dr. Holt."

He nodded. "The effect of a severe concussion can often take months to subside. What I need is plenty of rest. A few hours a day of serving the medical needs of these wonderful people, then a good deal of rest."

A knowing smile tugged at the corners of Jessie's mouth. She leaned close to the man's ear and whispered, "I know you, Doctor. Rest is not entirely what is on your mind."

He blushed. "Jessie, I think you had better go now," he said with a wink. "Because you read me entirely too well."

Jessie went back outside in the rain. An old woman threw a serape around her shoulders and took her hand to lead her to an adobe. Inside, a fire burned in a stone hearth and there was the usual delicious beans, tortillas, and corn. She was famished and so was Alvarado.

When they had eaten their fill, the old woman smiled and silently departed, leaving Jessie and the ex-lieutenant alone.

"Well, well," he said. "I like this already."

"I think you should go find another dry adobe where you can sleep," she said, noting that despite his appetite, there was still a hungry look to his dark, probing eyes.

Alvarado shrugged. "I think I like it here just fine. Over there is a nice straw mattress. The fire warms me and there is beauty whenever I look into your face."

She shook her head. "I'm sure my face is smeared with mud, my hair is matted and tangled, and I generally look like hell."

"You look magnificent," he said, coming over to take her into his arms. "You have filled my senses from the first moment we were together. I would have done anything for you."

"If the price was right," she said, looking up into his eyes. "You're not doing this for me or for the oppressed people of La Rosa. You're doing it for gold."

He pulled back, reached into his pockets, and extended her money. "Take it," he ordered. "Take it because I would rather be poor than to be held in your contempt."

146

Jessie ignored the money. She could see that he was not bluffing, that the mocking laughter she had thought to exist in his eyes was now gone, and that he was very earnest.

"If not money, then what do you want in repayment for delivery of those muskets and perhaps even the forfeit of your life?"

"I want you," he said. "I want you here and now."

Jessie turned her face up to his, and when they kissed, she felt her body shiver with desire. The exhaustion in her limbs fell away, and when he unbuttoned her blouse and paid homage to her breasts, she moaned with pleasure.

"You are a womanizer," she whispered as she quickly tore off the rest of her clothes, "a rascal and a man I do not entirely trust."

He chuckled low in his throat and kicked off his boots, then stood and removed his pants. She looked up and saw his great, throbbing erection, and she licked her lips with anticipation.

Alvarado knelt between her legs, and then he bent and paid attention to her breasts and her flat stomach. Then he found her honey pot.

"Ohhh," Jessie groaned as his tongue did wondrous things to her body. "Yes!"

Alvarado *was* a womanizer, and he knew how to play Jessie like a Mexican guitar. He took her up, made every fiber in her body tingle, then let her down slowly until she writhed with sweet agony.

"Don't . . . please," she begged, reaching for his manhood and pulling it down to rub it in her wetness.

Alvarado's body was hard and muscular. His dark skin gleamed in the firelight of the hearth, and his thick root looked black and immense as Jessie opened herself.

He filled her already yearning body, and yet she still could not get enough of him as their hips began to move together—slowly at first, then faster and faster until Jessie's fingernails

147

raked his buttocks and her lips drew back from her teeth.

"Now!" she cried as she felt her body jerk and flood itself in a tremendous shuddering climax. "Now!"

Alvarado was ready too. His pistoning hips seemed to drive through her, and when his body spasmed, she could feel the hot rush of his seed as he wildly emptied himself. He kept plunging in and out of her for what seemed like an eternity before Jessie went limp and Alvarado roared and collapsed to cover her.

It took Jessie several minutes to catch her breath. Her hands stroked his muscular buttocks, gently pulling him in and out of herself and feeling his manhood as it throbbed and diminished.

He lifted up on his elbows and then he gently kissed her mouth. "Have you ever had a real Mexican lover before?"

"I thought I had," she confessed, "but now I know better."

"I hope you are not too tired yet."

Jessie knew what he meant, and she wanted him again as soon as he was ready to take her.

"Jose," she whispered, "can you fight as well as you make love?"

"No." He chuckled. "But I can fight and I *will* fight even to the death for you."

"Not for me," she corrected, "for your people."

He rolled off of her, and his hands began to move over her body, which was now covered with their sweat. "What is this?" he asked, touching the almost healed wound on her ribs.

"It is nothing."

"It is a travesty on such a beautiful body as yours. I have had a few women in my time. Even more than a few. But never one looked or felt like you, Señorita Starbuck."

"I'll bet you tell that to all your conquests."

"Yes, but with you, I am sincere."

148

Jessie looked up into his face. "Tell me something and tell me the truth. This young dancer that your officer friends beat, causing you to kill them—was she also your lover?"

Jose Alvarado blinked, and after a long moment, he nodded. "How did you guess?"

"I don't know. I just did. And I think you were really in love with her, weren't you?"

He tried to laugh but failed. "You think too much," he finally said, his finger slipping down to caress the nub of her desire. "And I think you and I should talk less and make love more."

Jessie swallowed dryly, and without her being conscious of it, her hips began to squirm as his finger rekindled her passion.

"Tonight," she panted, crazy to have him mount her again, "I will will do as you say."

He chuckled. "But not tomorrow?"

"No," she breathed, "tomorrow, *I* give the orders and you follow them."

He fell upon her like a famished animal, and Jessie had no choice but to yield completely, content to let tomorrow take care of itself.

★

Chapter 19

Ki saw the Mexican boy come racing headlong down their lookout hill just to the north of La Rosa. Even before the breathless youth reached them, Ki turned to the suddenly frightened villagers and announced, "The Apache are coming. You all know what to do. Just act as if nothing has changed. If you've been frightened always before, act frightened now."

"That will be easy, Señor Ki," said a young man with terrible Apache-induced burn scars on his face, stomach, and legs.

Ki watched the villagers go to their preassigned places. The women began to grind corn, mend, and sew; the old men joined a circle and returned to spinning the old stories; and the young girls fled into the surrounding hills, where they had dug holes and would cover themselves with brush until the Indians departed.

Only the children showed anticipation. They had rehearsed this before, but now that the Apache were almost upon them, the children became terrified. Many cried, some ran to their mothers, and the older ones seemed suddenly numb, their faces blank masks that were even more disturbing than any display of outward fear.

Ki went to a child and picked the little fellow up. He was perhaps five years old, with large brown eyes and round cheeks, completely naked.

"Do not be afraid," Ki said to the child while its mother watched anxiously. "They will not hurt you this time."

The child sniffed and the samurai grinned as if he were happy. In truth, he was afraid, not for himself, but for these people who had been promised weapons yet undelivered, who had even started to believe that he, one man, could defy the fierce and ruthless Apache raiders.

The samurai handed the child over to his mother. He looked to the boy who had been on watch and had first seen the approaching Apache. Now, he asked the most vital question.

"How many?"

"Many!"

Ki nodded. Many might be ten or fifty, and he doubted that the frightened youth could accurately tell him the number. No matter. In a few minutes, he would see for himself, and then he would play this charade out however it went. If the Apache tried to steal slaves, he and the villagers were prepared to fight with arrows, sticks, spears, and knives. If the Apache had merely come to steal a little corn and a horse or a burro to eat, then there would be no resistance or bloodshed—this time.

Ki heard the sound of the Apache ponies before he saw them. He looked up, and suddenly, the Indians seemed to rise out from the depths of a barren ridge, and the samurai anxiously counted them one by one.

Twenty-one warriors. Far too many for these people to fight and hope to defeat with their primitive weapons. The Apache were heavily armed. They had repeating rifles stolen, no doubt, from north of the border. They were strong, confident, and seemingly invincible.

Ki steeled himself and let the peace in his heart spread through his limbs. He could not fight. He must be calm and brave. He must not anger the Apache this time unless they came for blood.

He stepped out alone to the edge of the village and watched the Apache come. They were small, square men, dark, dirty, and determined to have what they wanted. They hated the Mexicans, the gringos, and anyone not of their own culture. They loved to fight, they seemed not to feel pain the way others did, and they thrived on hardship. It was said that an Apache could run a hundred miles on bare feet through a scorching desert without food or even water. That he could survive where even coyotes starved. That he knew no fear of death or privation and had no more mercy than a bobcat. That he had the vision of the hawk and the heart of the mountain puma. That he killed, like a wild beast, out of a sheer joy.

Ki had fought Apache before and won. But he respected these hard, often cruel warriors as no others he had faced on the continent of North America.

The samurai closed his eyes and meditated, legs spread wide apart, arms hanging limp at his sides, without any visible weapons. He felt a deep stillness flow through his body, and his mind grew very calm, almost detached. He took several deep breaths, and the oxygen in his lungs gave him new strength. He felt very, very strong. If he should die within the next few minutes, death would come with honor and he would take the souls of many brave Apache with him into the next world.

Only when he could smell the dust of the Apache horses and feel the thunder of their hooves make the earth shake at his feet did Ki open his eyes. He folded his arms over his black tunic and felt the *shuriken* star blades. Hidden also in his tunic were the deadly *nunchaku*, two heavy sticks attached together at one end by a few inches of braided horsehair. The sticks were seven inches long, flat on only one side, where they fit together. With them, Ki could effectively perform virtually

152

every block or strike, and when he gripped one stick and whirled the other, the *nunchaku* could easily break skulls or shatter an enemy's forearms. Thrusts could smash his face or throat, and when the sticks were brought sharply together, they could crack fingers or any joint like a walnut in the jaws of a nutcracker.

The Indians drew in their ponies, and Ki was embroiled in a dust cloud. One of the Apache glared hatefully at him, then surveyed the village. He returned his eyes to the samurai, for he had never seen a man dressed like Ki. He spoke rapidly in Apache, and when Ki did not respond even to blink, he tried Spanish.

"Who are you!"

"I am samurai."

"You are a dead man."

"You speak strong, but you have many men to give you courage."

The Apache's dark skin tightened around the eyes. He dismounted and stepped out in front of his warriors. Sizing Ki up, he was not impressed, for he was the larger, broader man.

"I will kill you myself."

"And if I kill you instead, will your warriors go in peace, or will they shame your memory by doing to me what you could not?"

The Apache's lips drew back from his teeth. Ki saw the man's entire body shudder with rage, and his hand found the big knife at his side. It was a Bowie, heavy and enough to kill the courage of any opponent and gut him like a deer.

Ki tensed and lowered himself into a slight crouch. He raised his hands in the traditional fighting stance. The Apache was puzzled. He frowned, then barked something in his own language. A warrior tossed a knife, which came to a rest at Ki's feet.

"Pick it up," the warrior said. "I would not have my men see that I had any advantage over you."

"Don't worry about that," Ki said, "because you don't. I am samurai, a warrior from another world."

"There is no other world." The Apache began to circle Ki, a thin smile of contempt on his round, brutal face. "Except the one that you are about to visit."

Ki said nothing. He focused on the Apache's merciless eyes. He had seen more warmth in the eyes of a timber wolf. The Apache's hair was long, like the samurai's, and also tied back out of his eyes with braided leather. He wore moccasins, a breechcloth, and two sets of cartridge belts that crisscrossed his broad chest.

He feinted a thrust, which Ki ignored. His eyes tightened, for he had expected the samurai to be deceived and then lunge. The Apache kicked a little dirt at the samurai, then kicked more. The third time he kicked, he kicked high and his foot was aimed for Ki's crotch.

Ki spun and lashed out with a flat-foot kick, a powerful blow that caught the Apache in the solar plexus. The Indian's cheeks blew out and his eyes bulged with pain. He staggered backward, and the samurai attacked, hands striking face and arms. The Apache howled and then lashed out with the knife. It sliced the samurai across his chest, and a thin trickle of blood leaked into his severed tunic. The Apache hooted.

Ki stepped back. His opponent was no longer mocking him with a taunting smile. The Bowie knife was trembling slightly in the Indian's fist, and Ki knew that the man's forearm was numb from a knife-hand blow that had landed solidly. The wonder was that the Apache could even hold his knife, much less stand. Few men could have stood the terrible punishment of the first foot strike to the solar plexus, one of the most debilitating blows in the samurai's arsenal.

154

"Who are you?" the big Apache panted, trying but not quite able to mask his suffering.

"I am samurai."

"You are not a white man."

"Half-white, half-Japanese."

The Apache wiped his face of sweat. "You are about to die," he grunted, moving in again.

Ki retreated and the Apache hooted even louder, thinking Ki's courage had begun to bleed like the wound across his chest. Ki's opponent began to slash his knife back and forth. His eyes lost their pain and he grew bolder with each passing moment.

Ki found himself backed against an adobe. Out of the corner of his eyes, he could see the Mexican people, and they looked terrified.

"Now," the Apache said, "you will hang on the blade of my knife."

"I don't think so," Ki said, still and waiting.

The Apache lunged forward, left arm outstretched in case his opponent tried to jump sideways, right hand filled with the blood-tipped Bowie knife.

Ki did what the Apache would never have suspected. He threw himself forward, the iron-hard edge of his hand slashing downward to connect with the base of the Apache's thick neck. He tasted the Indian's foul breath, saw his eyes roll upward, and then he gave the Indian a hip-throw that brought him down hard in the dirt. Ki dropped one knee on the man's chest and snatched up the Bowie to place it at the Indian's throat.

The other Apache raised their rifles, but something in the samurai's eyes told them they would be signing their leader's death warrant if they opened fire.

It was a standoff.

For long seconds, the air snapped with tension. Ki waited, the knife drawing a little blood just as his chest bled. Finally,

155

one of the Apache spoke harshly to the others. He and two others dismounted, and dropping their rifles, they came forward to claim their fallen leader.

Ki dropped the Bowie and put his back to the wall. He understood that the mounted Apache could now riddle him with their bullets, but he was counting on a warrior's code of honor to spare his life, at least for the present.

The three Indians pulled their leader to his feet. He was out cold and had to be thrown over the back of his pony.

"We will kill you with bullets the next time we return," the Apache who had assumed command growled. "If you are still here, not only will *you* die, but so will many others!"

The villagers heard and they believed. They cringed in fear and an old woman began to wail. The Apache remounted and rode slowly away. In the cornfield, they dismounted and took what they wanted, casting challenging glances back at the village. At one place, a Mexican woman had dropped a basket of corn and ran. Now, the Apache took the corn, and one of them urinated in the basket to show his supreme contempt for the villagers.

"You must go away now!" a Mexican woman cried, but the girl named Conchita emerged from hiding and grew angry. "If he goes, the Apache will return and kill us all! Do not talk so stupid!"

Ki listened, but he did not speak until the people begged to to hear his opinion. And then he said, "I will stay until Señorita Starbuck and the doctor return with rifles, and when the Apache come again, we will surprise and kill them to the last man."

Conchita's eyes filled with pride. She hugged the samurai and fretted over the knife wound, which was little more than a scratch.

Turning to watch the Apache vanish over a distant hill, she spat in the dirt and her face twisted with hatred.

"Do not think of their cruelties," the samurai told her. "It is past."

"Will you really kill them all?" she asked loudly, so that the entire village could hear his answer.

"*We* with muskets will kill them if they come again," the samurai promised. "I cannot do it alone."

He raised his voice and said, "Once you have weapons, you must all learn to use them and find the heart to fight. It is the only way you will ever be free."

The people believed him, but nothing could hide their fear. And as they avoided his steady gaze, Ki wondered if—even armed—they would have the courage to stand up. And now, as he had a hundred times before, he turned to the south, eyes straining into the shimmering heat waves of the Sonoran Desert.

Where was Jessie? his heart cried out once again. Where?

★

Chapter 20

"There it is!" Jessie shouted, pulling the weapon-laden horse behind her and galloping on into La Rosa.

As soon as she and Jose Alvarado were spotted by the villagers, they shouted with happiness and came rushing forward. They saw the Mexican muskets, the keg of black powder, and the lead balls. Jessie felt their hands pat her legs as she rode anxiously into the village.

"Ki?"

He stepped out to greet her with a smile on his face. Jessie heaved a sigh of relief. "Thank heavens you and this village are all right! I was so afraid that the Apache would get here before we did."

Ki waited until she dismounted. "They did come," he said, noting the tall young Mexican wearing an officer's uniform bearing the insignia of a lieutenant. "But they went away again without taking anything more than a few ears of corn."

Conchita butted in. "This is not true! Ki have big fight with Apache leader. He could have killed him but let him live so they do not kill us!"

Jessie's smile died. "Is that right?"

Ki gave the barest hint of a nod. "They *will* be back," he said. "They promised they'd spill blood if I was here when they came."

"You aren't thinking that we should just give these people these muskets and ride north, are you?"

"Of course not. If we don't stay to train them, the muskets will be nearly useless." Ki looked to the officer sitting his horse next to Jessie. "I can see that we have a soldier and I'll bet he's the perfect one to do the training and the drills."

Alvarado looked the village over. "I hardly see any men of fighting age, Señor Samurai. I do not think these women and children—"

"We will fight to the death!" Conchita cried. "Just show us how to use the muskets and we will do the rest."

Alvarado studied the buxom peasant girl and a slow grin spread across his handsome face. "If this village had just one hundred pretty tigers like you, señorita, then they could defeat the entire army of Mexico!"

Conchita beamed. She pushed her breasts out proudly and placed her hands on her hips. Her dark eyes flashed. "You have a slick tongue, señor, but sweet talk is of no help to my village. What else can you do?"

"I can do many things," he said, dismounting and walking over to the packhorse. With everyone watching, he unwrapped and removed a musket, then quickly loaded the weapon and turned around. His black eyes roamed the village, and when he saw a cluster of small gourds hanging from a leather thong beside an adobe, he threw the musket to his shoulder, and without even seeming to aim, he pulled the trigger.

The musket roared, and one of the little gourds exploded into a thousand bits. The distance was a good fifty yards. A very impressive bit of marksmanship. Everyone cheered, and only Jessie and Ki wondered if the officer had actually taken aim on a single gourd or had simply tried to hit the mass.

Alvarado reloaded in silence, listening to the villagers chatter with excitement. When the musket was reloaded, he stepped over to Conchita. "Now your turn, my little fighting tiger."

"But I never shoot before!" she said, retreating a step.

"Then I will show you how," he said, stepping around behind her and enfolding her in his arms as he brought the musket to her shoulder. Jessie was amused to see how he pressed his hips to Conchita's buttocks and shifted just enough that she could not be certain if the movement was deliberately intended to stimulate her.

"Now," he whispered, "put your lovely cheek to the stock and I will show you how to hold the musket and aim."

They all watched as Conchita took aim with the lieutenant's help, and then he whispered into her ear, "Squeeze the trigger, pretty one. Pretend it is something that feels very good to the touch. Something that you love to caress or even fondle."

Jessie saw the pretty girl blush and the musket shook a bit more, but Alvarado steadied it.

"What am I supposed to shoot?" she asked.

"One of the other gourds," he said.

Conchita was trembling and the musket was heavy, but Alvarado grew serious and made her relax, then concentrate. "Squeeze, my little tiger. Caress the trigger."

The musket roared, and the cluster of gourds kicked high in the air as another was pulverized. The villagers shouted with approval and became very excited, Conchita most of all. She jumped up and down, then hugged Alvarado's neck and squealed with delight. "That is what I will do to an Apache!"

Alvarado held her longer and tighter than necessary, and when the man released her, Ki stepped forward and said, "Are you going to use that method to teach them all how to aim and shoot?"

Alvarado laughed outright. "No, Samurai Ki," he said with his broad smile. "Only that one. The others, I will train as I was taught to train the Mexican soldiers."

"Good," Ki said before walking away.

Jessie wondered if the samurai was actually jealous of the Mexican officer. However, since she had never seen him show the slightest hint of jealousy before, she decided he was simply annoyed at Alvarado for taking such bold liberties with Conchita in front of her people.

"We should start training at once," she said.

Alvarado agreed. "Why don't we unload these muskets and start right now."

"Good. Any idea how long it might take for these people to learn how to shoot straight?"

Alvarado looked around at the collection of old women, boys, girls, and old men. "Years," he finally said.

"We must do it in days," Jessie told the man. "Our own lives, as well as those of these people, demand it."

"I cannot make miracles," Alvarado said quietly. "These are not a fighting people."

"They will fight now," Jessie vowed. "And maybe if we had been subject to the cruelties of the Apache for generations, we would not be so brave either."

"Maybe," he said quietly. "At any rate, we will do the best that we can and I will stand beside you and the little tiger when the Apache come. Perhaps we will at least have the element of surprise on our side."

"Perhaps," Jessie said, privately wondering if anything could stand up to the Apache warriors who would come all too soon.

For the rest of that day and the next and the next, Jessie, Ki, and Lieutenant Alvarado worked furiously to prepare La Rosa to defend itself against the Apache. Ki took charge of helping each villager dig a hole for hiding in. Some of the holes were right in the middle of the cornfields and were covered up with brown stalks. Other holes were close to the little adobe houses in the village, or over by the small plaza or chapel. The idea,

Ki explained, was that everyone should hide at first warning and then, when the Apache entered their trap, lift up from a crouch, lay their muskets down on the lip of their hole, take aim, and fire.

"Shoot low for the bodies," he told them all. "And if you miss the man, you will at least hit his legs or the horse and he will fall. Their ponies will thrash and pin them or crush their legs. Remember, shoot low."

Alvarado agreed. He spent the first two days teaching the people, young and old alike, how to load, fire, and reload their muskets. He taught them how to clean the rifles, and he inspected them as if they were on parade in Mexico City.

The villagers were frightened but determined. When Alvarado and Jessie began to have them shoot for target practice, however, they were very reluctant to waste ammunition.

"It is not a waste!" Alvarado said one afternoon with exasperation. "You must shoot the targets so that you can learn how to hit what you aim for. Without practice, you will miss the Apache!"

The villagers listened, and they grudgingly shot the muskets, but they had been so poor so long, Jessie could see, that using valuable lead and black powder bothered them greatly.

"After we defeat the Apache," she said late one afternoon, "I will return to the United States and buy more lead and black powder to send down to your village."

"Do you swear this on the cross of Jesus?" an old woman wanted to know.

"Yes," Jessie promised. "I swear it on the cross of Jesus."

After that, the people of La Rosa did not hesitate to load, fire, and reload as often as Lieutenant Alvarado wanted.

Four days after their arrival, Jessie and the samurai walked up on the lookout hill and sat down. It was sunset and the kindest time of day in the Sonoran Desert. They studied the village below and saw Alvarado talking with Conchita.

162

"He will have her and then leave her one day," Jessie said.

Ki nodded. "Maybe and maybe not. She is quite a woman. The kind that grows on a man."

"Has she 'grown' on you?"

"A little," Ki conceded, "but my duty is and always will be to you."

"It doesn't have to be," she said earnestly. "Ki, if there is ever a time when you give your heart to another woman, I want—"

"No!" He lowered his voice. "I am sorry. But I am samurai and that can never change. Without my code of honor, I would be nothing."

"I don't agree," she said, placing her hand on his knee in as much a show of affection as she had ever expressed with him, "but you must do what you feel is right."

"They will come soon," Ki said. "I can feel the Apache coming now. Tonight, I will sleep here at this place."

Jessie nodded. "Tomorrow morning I will send up a boy to watch and you will come down for food and to rest."

Ki said nothing, which Jessie took to mean he was in agreement. She studied his face, then looked down at La Rosa fading in the dying sunlight. "Do they have a chance?"

"Yes. If I did not believe that, I would not stay."

Jessie felt reassured, and his confidence greatly lifted her flagging spirits. "Will they come tomorrow?"

"Maybe tomorrow."

She stood up, feeling very tired. "I will be glad to get this fight over with," she told the samurai. "I will be glad to get back to Texas."

"What about California?" he asked. "That was our destination."

"To hell with those business meetings," she told him. "Someone will make the right decisions. That's why I hire the best and pay the best."

Ki nodded. "Good night," he said.

"Good night."

Jessie walked down from the lookout hill and back into the village. She *was* tired, and she sensed that Ki believed that tomorrow the Apache would come again. And she hoped that he was correct in believing that when they did, the villagers of La Rosa would be equal to the fight.

All of their lives depended upon it because once the Apache were attacked, they would have to annihilate the village as an example to any others that might resist their deprivations. To do anything less than to kill every man, woman, and child in the little farming village below would be considered a sign of weakness.

And more than anything else, the Apache hated weakness.

★

Chapter 21

The Apache did come the next day. It was two hours after the noonday meal, when the villagers would have been expected to have their siesta. The sun was blazing and the heat was intense. Dogs panted, old women waved grass fans to cool their brows, and even the children huddled in the shade and seemed listless.

Ki's lookout spotted the Apache when they were still several miles away. The Indians rode without fear that any warning might be to their disadvantage. It probably never occurred to them that the poor Mexican people would ever dare to resist— why should they after generations of subjugation? Only occasionally did an individual Mexican display resistance, and he was rewarded with a lingering death.

"Everyone to their places!" Ki shouted.

Jessie checked a musket, reloaded supplies and her Colt revolver, and took her own place of hiding. Lieutenant Alvarado was cool and strode to an adobe. He had six Mexican muskets loaded and lined up side by side. Conchita would hand him a fresh one as soon as each was fired. She would also be reloading for him. Jessie figured that the lieutenant would kill many Apache this day.

Ki took his place in front of the village. A few feet to his rear was a deep manhole covered with reeds and dirt. Watching him stand so alone before the rapidly approaching Apache made Jessie's heart bang against her ribs with fear. She loved Ki like a brother and would have given her life to save him.

The Apache saw the samurai standing alone to face them, and they drew their horses in about a hundred yards from the village.

"You are a fool!" shouted the big warrior that Ki had beaten. "You should have gone away. I gave you that choice."

"As I gave you your life!" Ki shouted back.

"So," the Apache said, "we are even."

Jessie saw Ki nod his head. The air seemed dead and suddenly very oppressive. She found she was perspiring heavily, and she imagined the villagers, all crouched in their little holes, were sweating heavily too.

The leader raised his rifle and then looked at Ki with the same menacing expression an eagle might before it swooped down to skewer a rabbit with its great talons. Then, the man howled and slapped the rifle down across the rump of his pony. The animal bolted forward, and the Apache came charging in at Ki, firing their weapons.

Ki waited a moment; then he stepped back and dropped into his hole, to the great amazement of the Apache, whose shouts died on their lips. They were even more astonished a moment later when the samurai reappeared with a musket, took aim, and fired. Jessie blinked to see the leader's chest sprout a rose.

For La Rosa, she thought as the Apache swept forward, repeating rifles crashing.

Lieutenant Alvarado opened fire next. His initial volley sent another Apache tumbling from his horse, and suddenly, heads and rifles began to pop up all over the village.

The Apache, despite their fierceness and superior weaponry, were caught in a terrible crossfire. Many horses went down, squealing in death and falling on their riders. In two instances,

Jessie saw old men and women actually crawl out of the holes to run forward and club the helpless Apache as they lay pinned under their thrashing horses.

The battle could not have lasted more than three or four minutes. Alvarado killed six Apache with six musket blasts, and Conchita's hands flew to reload his weapons. She needn't have bothered, however. Ki killed the last of the fallen warriors with his hands, and the village immediately fell into a silence.

Horses were caught and calmed. Those that were mortally wounded were blessed and then put out of their misery. The people of La Rosa kept walking around the bodies of the fallen Apache as if they could not believe what they themselves had helped to do.

"It is over," Jessie told them. "We must now bury the dead."

"And pray!" an old woman cried, turning her face up to the sky. "Pray to God for delivering his faithful!"

Jessie smiled. "That too."

Conchita came over to throw her arms around the samurai. She began to cry.

"What is wrong?" he asked.

"I am so happy to be the ones who are alive. We lost no one this day!"

"You must make sure that the people of this village never forget what happened here and that they always remain vigilant. Only that way can you be always free."

"But these people are farmers! We are not fighters."

Jose Alvarado came over to her. "I will stay and teach them to become both," he promised.

"No Texas?" Jessie asked, remembering how she had promised this man a job.

"No," he said, "but I would like the rest of the money you promised to pay me."

"You will have it even if I have to deliver it personally."

Ki shot Jessie a questioning glance that left little doubt in her mind that he would think her crazy if she ever came this far down into Mexico and the Apache country again.

"However," Jessie quickly amended, "I do not expect that that will ever be necessary. I will make sure that I give the money and the black powder I promised to someone that I can trust."

"When it comes to money, you can never trust anyone," Alvarado said. "But I promise that I will stay in this place until these brave people can always defend themselves."

"Maybe the half-breed named Juara Madrid will one day become a famous leader and make a lasting peace for the Apache."

Alvarado snorted with derision. "And maybe one day horses will sprout wings and fly."

Jessie shrugged her shoulders, knowing that Jose Alvarado might never trust the Apache or see them live side by side with the Mexicans in peace.

She walked over to one of the Apache ponies. "Does this animal look like it will carry me to Texas?" she asked the samurai.

"I think so," Ki said.

Jessie motioned toward a second pony. "That one looks like it might carry you as well. Why don't we find out?"

"Right now?"

"Yes," Jessie said, her eyes moving over the grateful people and twenty-one dead Apache. "Right now."

Ki jumped on his horse before Conchita could start to raise a fuss and perhaps even cling to him and embarrass them both. He heard her call his name, and he turned to wave good-bye, only to see that Jose Alvarado's arm was encircling her small waist.

Tonight, Alvarado would find out what kind of a woman Conchita really was, and he might stay in La Rosa forever. Ki hoped so. A little more fighting blood would be very good for these humble people.

Fury knew something was wrong long before he saw the wagon train spread out, unmoving, across the plains in front of him.

From miles away, he had noticed the cloud of dust kicked up by the hooves of the mules and oxen pulling the wagons. Then he had seen that tan-colored pall stop and gradually be blown away by the ceaseless prairie wind.

It was the middle of the afternoon, much too early for a wagon train to be stopping for the day. Now, as Fury topped a small, grass-covered ridge and saw the motionless wagons about half a mile away, he wondered just what kind of damn fool was in charge of the train.

Stopping out in the open without even forming into a circle was like issuing an invitation to the Sioux, the Cheyenne, or the Pawnee. War parties roamed these plains all the time just looking for a situation as tempting as this one.

Fury reined in, leaned forward in his saddle, and thought about it. Nothing said he had to go help those pilgrims. They might not even want his help.

But from the looks of things, they needed his help, whether they wanted it or not.

He heeled the rangy lineback dun into a trot toward the wagons. As he approached, he saw figures scurrying back and forth around the canvas-topped vehicles. Looked sort of like an anthill after someone stomped it.

Fury pulled the dun to a stop about twenty feet from the lead wagon. Near it, a man was stretched out on the ground with so many men and women gathered around him that Fury could only catch a glimpse of him through the crowd. When some of the men turned to look at him, Fury said, "Howdy. Thought it looked like you were having trouble."

"Damn right, mister," one of the pilgrims snapped. "And if you're of a mind to give us more, I'd advise against it."

Fury crossed his hands on the saddlehorn and shifted in the saddle, easing his tired muscles. "I'm not looking to cause trouble for anybody," he said mildly.

He supposed he might appear a little threatening to a bunch of immigrants who until now had never been any farther west than the Mississippi. Several days had passed since his face had known the touch of the razor, and his rough-hewn features could be a little intimidating even without the beard stubble. Besides that, he was well armed with a Colt's Third Model Dragoon pistol holstered on his right hip, a Bowie knife sheathed on his left, and a Sharps carbine in the saddleboot under his right thigh. And he had the look of a man who knew how to use all three weapons.

A husky, broad-shouldered six-footer, John Fury's height was apparent even on horseback. He wore a broad-brimmed, flat-crowned black hat, a blue work shirt, and fringed buckskin pants that were tucked into high-topped black boots. As he swung down from the saddle, a man's voice, husky with strain, called out, "Who's that? Who are you?"

The crowd parted, and Fury got a better look at the figure on the ground. It was obvious that he was the one who had spoken. There was blood on the man's face, and from the twisted look of him as he lay on the ground, he was busted up badly inside.

Fury let the dun's reins trail on the ground, confident that the horse wouldn't go anywhere. He walked over to the injured man and crouched beside him. "Name's John Fury," he said.

The man's breath hissed between his teeth, whether in pain or surprise Fury couldn't have said. "Fury? I heard of you."

Fury just nodded. Quite a few people reacted that way when they heard his name.

"I'm . . . Leander Crofton. Wagonmaster of . . . this here train." The man struggled to speak. He appeared to be in his fifties and had a short, grizzled beard and the leathery skin of a man who had spent nearly his whole life outdoors. His pale blue eyes were narrowed in a permanent squint.

"What happened to you?" Fury asked.

"It was a terrible accident— " began one of the men standing nearby, but he fell silent when Fury cast a hard glance at him. Fury had asked Crofton, and that was who he looked toward for the answer.

Crofton smiled a little, even though it cost him an effort. "Pulled a damn fool stunt," he said. "Horse nearly stepped on a rattler, and I let it rear up and get away from me. Never figured the critter'd spook so easy." The wagonmaster paused to draw a breath. The air rattled in his throat and chest. "Tossed me off and stomped all over me. Not the first time I been stepped on by a horse, but then a couple of the oxen pullin' the lead wagon got me, too, 'fore the driver could get 'em stopped."

"God forgive me, I . . . I am so sorry." The words came in a tortured voice from a small man with dark curly hair and a beard. He was looking down at Crofton with lines of misery etched onto his face.

"Wasn't your fault, Leo," Crofton said. "Just . . . bad luck."

Fury had seen men before who had been trampled by horses. Crofton was in a bad way, and Fury could tell by the look in the man's eyes that Crofton was well aware of it. The wagonmaster's chances were pretty slim.

"Mind if I look you over?" Fury asked. Maybe he could do something to make Crofton's passing a little easier, anyway.

One of the other men spoke before Crofton had a chance to answer. "Are you a doctor, sir?" he asked.

Fury glanced up at him, saw a slender, middle-aged man with iron-gray hair. "No, but I've patched up quite a few hurt men in my time."

"Well, I am a doctor," the gray-haired man said. "And I'd appreciate it if you wouldn't try to move or examine Mr. Crofton. I've already done that, and I've given him some laudanum to ease the pain."

Fury nodded. He had been about to suggest a shot of whiskey, but the laudanum would probably work better.

Crofton's voice was already slower and more drowsy from the drug as he said, "Fury . . ."

"Right here."

"I got to be sure about something . . . You said your name was . . . John Fury."

"That's right."

"The same John Fury who . . . rode with Fremont and Kit Carson?"

"I know them," Fury said simply.

"And had a run-in with Cougar Johnson in Santa Fe?"

"Yes."

"Traded slugs with Hemp Collier in San Antone last year?"

"He started the fight, didn't give me much choice but to finish it."

"Thought so." Crofton's hand lifted and clutched weakly at Fury's sleeve. "You got to . . . make me a promise."

Fury didn't like the sound of that. Promises made to dying men usually led to a hell of a lot of trouble.

Crofton went on, "You got to give me . . . your word . . . that you'll take these folks through . . . to where they're goin'."

"I'm no wagonmaster," Fury said.

"You know the frontier," Crofton insisted. Anger gave him strength, made him rally enough to lift his head from the ground and glare at Fury. "You can get 'em through. I know you can."

"Don't excite him," warned the gray-haired doctor.

"Why the hell not?" Fury snapped, glancing up at the physician. He noticed now that the man had his arm around the shoulders of a pretty red-headed girl in her teens, probably his daughter. He went on, "What harm's it going to do?"

The girl exclaimed, "Oh! How can you be so . . . so callous?"

Crofton said, "Fury's just bein' practical, Carrie. He knows we got to . . . got to hash this out now. Only chance we'll get." He looked at Fury again. "I can't make you promise, but it . . . it'd sure set my mind at ease while I'm passin' over if I knew you'd take care of these folks."

Fury sighed. It was rare for him to promise anything to anybody. Giving your word was a quick way of getting in over your head in somebody else's problems. But Crofton was dying, and even though they had never crossed paths before, Fury recognized in the old man a fellow Westerner.

"All right," he said.

A little shudder ran through Crofton's battered body, and he rested his head back against the grassy ground. "Thanks," he said, the word gusting out of him along with a ragged breath.

"Where are you headed?" Fury figured the immigrants could tell him, but he wanted to hear the destination from Crofton.

"Colorado Territory . . . Folks figure to start 'em a town . . . somewhere on the South Platte. Won't be hard for you to find . . . a good place."

No, it wouldn't, Fury thought. No wagon train journey could be called easy, but at least this one wouldn't have to deal with crossing mountains, just prairie. Prairie filled with savages and outlaws, that is.

179

A grim smile plucked at Fury's mouth as that thought crossed his mind. "Anything else you need to tell me?" he asked Crofton.

The wagonmaster shook his head and let his eyelids slide closed. "Nope. Figger I'll rest a spell now. We can talk again later."

"Sure," Fury said softly, knowing that in all likelihood, Leander Crofton would never wake up from this rest.

Less than a minute later, Crofton coughed suddenly, a wracking sound. His head twisted to the side, and blood welled for a few seconds from the corner of his mouth. Fury heard some of the women in the crowd cry out and turn away, and he suspected some of the men did, too.

"Well, that's all," he said, straightening easily from his kneeling position beside Crofton's body. He looked at the doctor. The red-headed teenager had her face pressed to the front of her father's shirt and her shoulders were shaking with sobs. She wasn't the only one crying, and even the ones who were dry-eyed still looked plenty grim.

"We'll have a funeral service as soon as a grave is dug," said the doctor. "Then I suppose we'll be moving on. You should know, Mr. . . . Fury, was it? You should know that none of us will hold you to that promise you made to Mr. Crofton."

Fury shrugged. "Didn't ask if you intended to or not. I'm the one who made the promise. Reckon I'll keep it."

He saw surprise on some of the faces watching him. All of these travelers had probably figured him for some sort of drifter. Well, that was fair enough. Drifting was what he did best.

But that didn't mean he was a man who ignored promises. He had given his word, and there was no way he could back out now.

He met the startled stare of the doctor and went on, "Who's the captain here? You?"

180

"No, I . . . You see, we hadn't gotten around to electing a captain yet. We only left Independence a couple of weeks ago, and we were all happy with the leadership of Mr. Crofton. We didn't see the need to select a captain."

Crofton should have insisted on it, Fury thought with a grimace. You never could tell when trouble would pop up. Crofton's body lying on the ground was grisly proof of that.

Fury looked around at the crowd. From the number of people standing there, he figured most of the wagons in the train were at least represented in this gathering. Lifting his voice, he said, "You all heard what Crofton asked me to do. I gave him my word I'd take over this wagon train and get it on through to Colorado Territory. Anybody got any objection to that?"

His gaze moved over the faces of the men and women who were standing and looking silently back at him. The silence was awkward and heavy. No one was objecting, but Fury could tell they weren't too happy with this unexpected turn of events.

Well, he thought, when he had rolled out of his soogans that morning, he hadn't expected to be in charge of a wagon train full of strangers before the day was over.

The gray-haired doctor was the first one to find his voice. "We can't speak for everyone on the train, Mr. Fury," he said. "But I don't know you, sir, and I have some reservations about turning over the welfare of my daughter and myself to a total stranger."

Several others in the crowd nodded in agreement with the sentiment expressed by the physician.

"Crofton knew me."

"He knew you have a reputation as some sort of gunman!"

Fury took a deep breath and wished to hell he had come along after Crofton was already dead. Then he wouldn't be saddled with a pledge to take care of these people.

"I'm not wanted by the law," he said. "That's more than a

181

lot of men out here on the frontier can say, especially those who have been here for as long as I have. Like I said, I'm not looking to cause trouble. I was riding along and minding my own business when I came across you people. There's too many of you for me to fight. You want to start out toward Colorado on your own, I can't stop you. But you're going to have to learn a hell of a lot in a hurry."

"What do you mean by that?"

Fury smiled grimly. "For one thing, if you stop spread out like this, you're making a target of yourselves for every Indian in these parts who wants a few fresh scalps for his lodge." He looked pointedly at the long red hair of the doctor's daughter. Carrie—that was what Crofton had called her, Fury remembered.

Her father paled a little, and another man said, "I didn't think there was any Indians this far east." Other murmurs of concern came from the crowd.

Fury knew he had gotten through to them. But before any of them had a chance to say that he should honor his promise to Crofton and take over, the sound of hoofbeats made him turn quickly.

A man was riding hard toward the wagon train from the west, leaning over the neck of his horse and urging it on to greater speed. The brim of his hat was blown back by the wind of his passage, and Fury saw anxious, dark brown features underneath it. The newcomer galloped up to the crowd gathered next to the lead wagon, hauled his lathered mount to a halt, and dropped lithely from the saddle. His eyes went wide with shock when he saw Crofton's body on the ground, and then his gaze flicked to Fury.

"You son of a bitch!" he howled.

And his hand darted toward the gun holstered on his hip.